Montgomery Lake High #1

The Right Person

Written by Stacy A. Padula

Briley & Baxter Publications | Plymouth, Massachusetts

Paperback ISBN: 978-1-7350168-4-9
Hardcover ISBN: 978-1-7331536-5-2

Book Design: Stacy O'Halloran

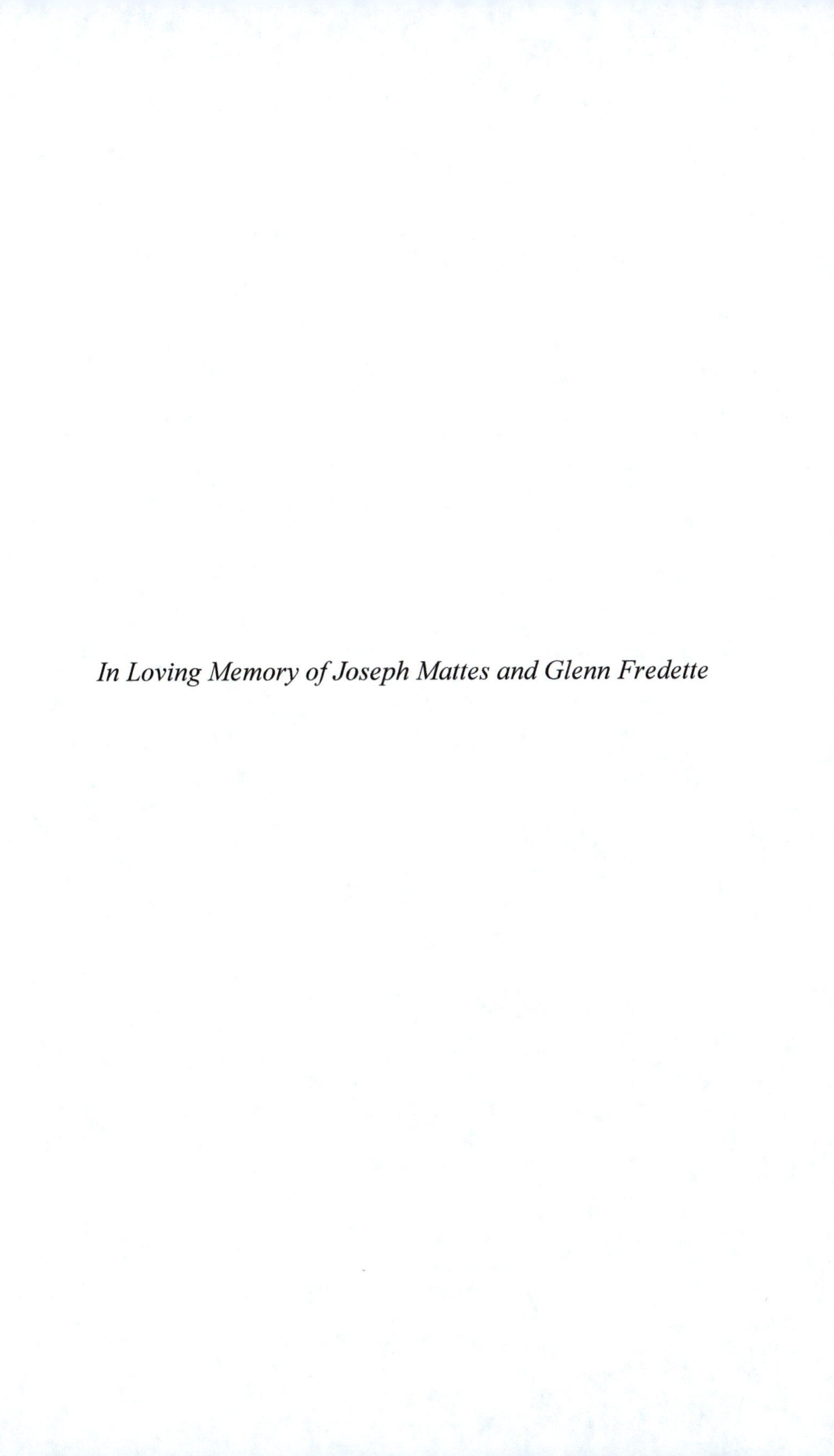

In Loving Memory of Joseph Mattes and Glenn Fredette

Meet the Characters

1st: Chris, Cathy, Jason, Chantal
2nd: Andy, Alyssa, Marc, Lisa
3rd: Courtney, Jon, Bobby, Marielle
4th: Bryan, Katherine, Leslie, Julianna

PREFACE

I was thirteen years old when I wrote the first draft of *The Right Person*. After being assigned a project on peer pressure in my eighth-grade health class, I decided to write this book, shocking my teacher when I handed in a ninety-page "essay."

At that moment, I had no idea that the Montgomery Lake High characters would remain a part of my life for years to come. What I did know, however, was that there was a need for realistic teen books—books that depict the social struggles of adolescence, books that aren't afraid to address drug abuse, sex, and moral convictions, books that would help prepare kids for the social battleground that is high school. I had searched high and low for books like that, and no matter how many I read, nothing prepared me for what I faced as a teenager. So, I kept writing and completed the first drafts of three of the Montgomery Lake High books before graduating high school.

After college, I stumbled upon my drafts of *The Right Person, When Darkness Tries to Hide,* and *The Forces Within.* Deciding the books could possibly help kids socially prepare for high school, I completed the series and sought a literary agent. From 2010-2014, the first editions of all five Montgomery Lake High books were published. When Barnes & Noble chose me as a featured author for its Teen Book Festival in 2016, I was in awe that the stories I wrote as a teenager were being embraced by strangers and sold in a mainstream bookstore.

This version you are now reading is the third edition of *The Right Person.* Minor updates have been made over the years, but the heart of the story has remained the same. Now, as the author of thirteen books and the founder of a publishing company, it is tempting to edit this book to include my professional writer's voice, but the power of this novel rests in that it was written by someone right in the midst of adolescence. Its teenage writing style is something it cannot lose without losing its intended purpose.

Sincerely,
Stacy A. Padula

PROLOGUE

<u>Chris Dunkin</u>

Just shy of my fifteenth birthday, I came to terms with the fact that I was a teenage alcoholic with a pretty serious drug problem. As you can presume, I was traveling fast down the road to destruction. This story my friends and I are about to tell you is important because, living it, I learned the true value of my life. It's somewhat of a teenage love story—packed tightly, of course, with all the unimportant drama you'd expect from high school freshmen—but more importantly it is a story of trial, inspiration, revelation, and death.

I'm asking you now to consider the possibility of death shining in a positive light. It's hard to imagine, I know; but as the truth unravels before your eyes (as it did before my own), you will see how experiencing death is the only chance we have of living. I ask you to read with an open mind. You will soon be in the shoes of high school freshmen, when every small bump in the road seems life jeopardizing. Perhaps you're yet to be there, or perhaps you've already been; either way, you must understand most importantly that this is a story about the greatest love of all. The pessimists may say it is impossible for a teenager to comprehend the depth of such love. I believe it is impossible for anyone of any age to comprehend, and I tell you this comfortably from an optimistic point of view.

"Love bears all things,
believes all things,
hopes all things,
and endures all things."

Chapter 1

The world stopped turning, the waves stopped crashing, and the fire stopped dancing as Chris Dunkin laid his eyes on her. He blinked, realizing somehow his life had just been changed. She had arrived at Saquish Beach with her boyfriend and taken a seat across the bonfire. Through the smoke of the fire, Chris studied the girl, attempting to understand why his stomach had lunged into flutters. Her dark hair was pulled back into a loose ponytail with a few stray locks framing her makeup-less face. She wore a gray hooded sweatshirt, a jean skirt, and white flip-flops—similar to what every girl at the party wore. From across the fire, there seemed to be nothing extraordinary about her physical appearance.

Jason Davids nudged Chris and then nodded towards the girl. "Courtney's hot, huh?" he said with wide eyes.

"She's all right," Chris replied, locking his eyes again on the girl Jason had called Courtney.

"That's Mayor Angeletti's daughter," Jason said. "She's more than all right, dude! I'd capitalize on her in a second if she weren't dating Sartelli. Now we know why he kept her hidden for so long."

Chris's eyes traveled to Bryan Sartelli, who was sitting on the log beside Courtney. Bryan was a good friend of Chris's, one whom he valued highly. As Chris's eyes shot back to Courtney's face, he began wondering if his mind was playing tricks on him. How could the sight of someone he'd never met floor him? Were his palms suddenly sweating profusely because of the heat from the nearby fire? Why was his heart pounding so heavily against his muscular chest? Would seeing her for the first time have taken such a tight grip on his heart if he hadn't been high? Yes, he believed it would have.

"I need to go talk to her," Chris said, while standing up from his seat suddenly.

Jason looked up at Chris in surprise, and then, slowly rose to meet his best friend. "All right, guy. I'll introduce you," he offered, leading Chris over to where Courtney was seated.

She looked up and smiled at Jason as he appeared before her. It was then that Chris noticed the sparkle in her sky-blue eyes. Studying her face up close, Chris was surprised by how attractive he found her features. From across the fire he had not recognized Courtney's beauty, yet he had still been undeniably drawn to her.

"Hello, Courtney. This is Chris," Jason greeted her. "He's a friend of Bryan's, too."

"Yeah, he's the guy we go to when we want to have some *fun*," Bryan explained to his girlfriend as he stood up to slap hands with Chris and Jason.

"It's nice to meet you," Courtney replied softly, dragging her eyes off Jason and planting them on Chris.

The flutters returned inside Chris's stomach, and he found himself unable to form any words in return. He smiled, nodded, and then walked past Bryan towards the Atlantic. It was low tide, and the bonfire was ten yards behind Chris when he sat down on the cool ground. Staring blankly at the waves crashing fifteen feet in front of him, Chris took off his sandals and pressed his feet deeply into the moist sand. A moment later, Courtney appeared beside him. She also took off her shoes and buried her feet in the sand. At that moment, all the stars seemed to align. Although their time alone only lasted a few seconds before Bryan and Jason joined them by the shore, for the first time in his life, Chris felt like he was in the right place at the right time.

CHAPTER 2

***

Two Months Later

The first bell of her high school career was an hour away from ringing. Courtney Angeletti stood before her mahogany framed full-length mirror, carefully examining her reflection. Her pearly white smile broadened, and her bright aquamarine eyes glistened as she thought of the friends she would soon be with.

As Courtney ventured through her Victorian bedroom suite, her white gold jewelry shimmered in all directions. Sunlight poured into her room as she approached the sliding glass door that led to her private balcony. A gentle breeze blew against Courtney's soft skin as she stepped outside and glanced at the town below. She reflected on her summer, Bryan, and the new friends she had made. She thought of the first time she met Chris Dunkin and how much her life had changed as a result. Although she felt guilty for breaking up with Bryan so suddenly, she was trying to ignore the sting in her heart. Two months prior, Chris had captivated her.

Before dating Chris, Courtney had been very involved in her church. Lately, she found herself struggling to make it there on Sundays, let alone to youth group on Fridays. Initially, she had thought God was drawing her toward Chris. After getting to know him, she was having second thoughts.

Truthfully, Courtney had found Bryan somewhat boring, and the idea of dating a "party-kid" like Chris had sounded exciting. No matter how hard she tried to convince herself that that had been the basis of her decision, she knew it was not the truth. After two months, she still could not understand the force that had overcome her and moved her to break up with Bryan.

⚜

In a home just a few miles away from Courtney's, Mrs. Sartelli hollered down the hallway for the third time that morning, "Bryan, get up!"

"I am," Bryan mumbled, placing his head beneath two pillows. Why was he so tired? As he started to wake up, flashbacks of Chris's party flooded his mind. *How could my parents have let me stay out so late on a school night?* Bryan ruminated while climbing out of his bed. *Oh, yeah, they didn't.* Chris's party had begun at midnight when his parents thought he was asleep, not getting wasted.

"I hate school," Bryan muttered, stumbling to stand up straight. His room spun when he tried to focus on his clock.

The numbers blurred together, and he realized he was still drunk.

"Bryan!" his mother screeched. "I want you down here, ready, in two minutes!"

Quickly Bryan threw a pair of khaki cargo pants over his flannel boxers. Tripping over one of his brown leather sandals, he reached for a gray GAP t-shirt that hung around his bedpost. He quickly threw on deodorant, cologne, the shirt, and his sandals, once again tripping over something or other.

⁂

Jon Anderson, another soon-to-be freshman at Montgomery Lake High, woke up at seven o'clock, thankful he had not gotten drunk the night before. Although he had attended his best friend Chris's party, he had not felt the desire to do anything in which his friends had indulged. Although Jon hung out with a crew known for throwing wild parties, experimenting with drugs, and stirring up trouble, he liked to think of himself differently. Chris, Jason, and Bryan had been his best friends since their idea of partying was eating Hoodsie Cups.

Jon dressed in his usual attire: a button-up Abercrombie dress shirt, jeans, and shell-toe sneakers. He brushed his teeth, washed his face, and spiked his short blond hair before heading downstairs to have breakfast with his younger sister and brother. After making them oatmeal, Jon only had time to grab a power bar to eat on the bus. He was fine with that; after staying up until 3:30 a.m., he could definitely use the energy.

In a mansion across Montgomery, Jason Davids had finally fallen asleep around five-thirty that morning. At the sound of his mother's voice calling him down to breakfast, he shot his large blue eyes wide open. It was only seven o'clock, but he felt wide awake.

Quickly, he made his way over to the bureau on which he had laid out his clothing the previous night. He threw on his freshly ironed khakis and green striped dress shirt, allowing it to hang loosely in front of his pants. Jason was a firm believer in dressing up for all occasions, even the first day of school. It probably had something to do with the fact that he had never seen either of his parents wear jeans. His father was a lawyer, and his mother was an interior designer, so they always dressed professionally. Jason, like his parents, was more comfortable looking good than wearing casual clothing. Before running downstairs to eat breakfast with his family, he glanced at his reflection. Wonderful—his pupils were back to their normal size.

At the Dunkin residence, Chris was yet to stir.

"Chris, get up!" his younger sister Katie squeaked as she flicked his bedroom light switch on and off.

"Go away!" Chris demanded while stuffing his messy, blond head of hair beneath his pillow.

"It's the first day of school! You have to go!" Katie exclaimed and walked to his bedside. "Come on," she pleaded and tugged on his muscular arm.

Chris groaned as he pulled his head out from under his pillow. "What time is it?" he mumbled and creased open his bloodshot, blue eyes.

"Seven-twenty," Katie replied angrily.

"@#$%," Chris muttered beneath his breath. Looking down, he realized he was still dressed in his clothes from the previous day. *What the heck happened last night?*

"You know, your friends ate all the food Mom and Dad left for us," Katie said. "That was our food for the next ten days!"

"Huh?" Chris asked and gazed at his sister in a confused manner.

Katie peered at him strangely. "Are you sick?"

Chris sighed. He had no interest in explaining the severity of his hangover to his eleven-year-old sister. "Come on. Let's find something for breakfast," he said and led her out of his messy bedroom.

Although the upstairs hallway looked clean, the hardwood floor felt sticky beneath Chris's bare feet. "Is Marc here?" he asked, referring to their older cousin who sometimes housesat when their parents went away.

"No," Katie responded flatly. "You don't remember him leaving last night? *I* do. Because *I* was still awake. Because *your friends* were so loud!"

Chris let out a heavy breath and began descending the stairs. Halfway down, he leaned over the railing and caught a glimpse at the party debris scattered throughout the living room. He halted on his step.

"If you're wondering, your friends did that, too," Katie said as she continued past him down the stairs. "You don't remember, do you?"

Chris rolled his eyes and proceeded after her. "Yeah, now I remember," he muttered.

"No, you don't!" Katie cried. "You never remember anymore! I saw you last night. Don't think I didn't. I see you all the time, smoking and drinking. You're a mess!"

"You don't know what you see," Chris retorted before tripping over an empty beer ball that lay on the living room floor.

"You're such a loser," Katie stated in such a disgusted manner that Chris's heart sank to his stomach.

CHAPTER 3

Although Courtney was physically seated in homeroom, she was mentally in another place: back at Chris's party, laughing at his foolish antics and socializing with his friends. Recently, Courtney had felt the desire to rebel tug at her heartstrings. At Chris's party, she took her first step in that direction. Although she did not drink any of the alcohol present at the party, she had felt satisfied just being in attendance. Even though Bryan and Chris were part of the same social circle, Bryan had always chosen time with Courtney over the partying scene. Since she began dating Chris, she had become a part of their inner circle—finally!

Montgomery Lake High was made up of students from all three Montgomery middle schools: Hamilton, Sterling, and Montgomery Lake. Courtney was well acquainted with everyone from Hamilton, where she had been her grade's vice president. She had accrued ties to the other two middle schools by hanging out with Chris. Chris and his best friend Jon had attended Montgomery Lake. Jason, Chris's other best friend, had studied at a private school, but his girlfriend, Cathy Kagelli, had gone to Sterling.

Courtney was trying to become friends with Cathy, a socialite of Chris's crew. Being Chris Dunkin's girlfriend won Courtney favor in the eyes of many, but it did not seem to win her any points with Cathy. Cathy was beautiful, powerful, and seemingly aware that she possessed both attributes. As Jason Davids' girlfriend, she could run the show without much opposition. Courtney was not sure if Cathy liked having another girl in her crew or if she viewed Courtney as a threat. Courtney didn't want to compete for popularity; she just wanted fun friends.

Truthfully, Courtney felt guilty about avoiding her childhood best friend, Julianna Camen, for the last few weeks. Nevertheless, she had decided that fitting in with Chris's crew should be her main priority. In order to be accepted by them, Courtney could not associate with a goody-goody like Julianna. Quite frankly, Julianna had nothing in common with Courtney's new friends and very little in common with Courtney, aside from ten years of friendship. Once she began dating Chris, Courtney had made a lot of adjustments to her lifestyle. Unfortunately for Julianna, she happened to be one of them.

"Hey, Angeletti!" Jon Anderson yelled from across Courtney's homeroom. Everyone looked Jon's way except for Courtney. "Court!" he shouted as he walked over to her desk.

"Huh?" Courtney asked, startled as she came out of her daze. "Oh! Hi."

"Hey," he smiled, taking a seat beside her. "Um, Chris told me to give you this," he said, referring to the note he had just thrown on her desk. "It's nothing bad, so don't worry. Oh, I'll introduce you to Alyssa at lunch. Sorry she couldn't make it last night. I'm looking forward to introducing you guys."

"Can't wait," Courtney said, while staring into Jon's chocolate-brown eyes. "You look awfully tired. You should go home today and rest. Chris is having another party tomorrow night, so I'm going to sleep all day after school."

"Nah," Jon said and shook his head. "I'm used to this by now."

<hr>

"JD, my man, what's up?!" Chris called out loudly as he entered his homeroom.

"Hey!" Jason greeted him, slapping hands with his best bud. "Nice party last night."

"Was it?" Chris asked. "I don't remember it at all. We destroyed my house. It's completely foodless. I feel really bad for Katie," he admitted in a somber tone.

Jason eyed Chris strangely. "And you're having another one tomorrow night?"

"Did I say that?" Chris asked, shaking his head in disgust.

"Yeah, dude! After everyone killed the last beer ball," Jason laughed, patting Chris on the back. "Wow! You really did have a rough night. Geez!"

"My sister said she saw me at the party," Chris said

and glanced at the floor. "I didn't do anything too terrible, did I?"

Jason laughed. "You're asking the wrong person, bro," he replied. "I dropped a few tabs with you early last night. I have no freakin' clue how I made it home in one piece. You're always the life of our parties, guy. That's a rep you should want to keep."

Staring blankly at his best friend's tired face, Chris reflected upon himself. For the past two years, he had been "the life of the party." Scary — he had no idea he had tripped the night before. He must have been completely wasted when he agreed to take acid on a school night. Finding out he had mixed acid with alcohol — and God knows what else — explained why Chris had blacked-out.

What Katie had said earlier when Chris was leaving for school sharply pierced his heart. He absolutely hated the person he had become: a terrible brother, an alcoholic, a user, and an emotionally disconnected boyfriend. He had begun to think there could be more to life than partying and getting high. He wanted to escape from his life, but he was in over his head. While dating Courtney, he had managed to abstain from taking most of the hard drugs he had experimented with in the past. However, weed and alcohol were still large parts of his life. He felt dependent on both vices. How had he sunk to that level? Worse, how could he get out? These thoughts had been haunting his mind for the last few months.

Chris did not want Courtney to get pulled into his clique. He liked her the way she was — innocent, pure, and full of respectable values. The rumors were true; his friends were wild. In fact, Chris was beginning to hate his social life as much as his academic world. That was another problem. In the past year, his grades had dropped from A's and B's to C's. At football camp over the summer, MLH's JV coach told Chris he might want him on the team, which was unheard of for a freshman. That would require Chris to maintain a certain GPA and pass periodic drug tests. Since Peewee football, Chris had been told by his coaches that he was blessed with the same athletic talent as his Uncle Jack and his cousins, Taylor and Jordan—all MLH legends. With football, Katie, and Courtney in mind, he knew it was time to clean up his act.

"Dunkin, are you with me?" Jason asked, waving his hand before Chris's face.

"Huh?" Chris questioned him, escaping from his daze. "What?"

"Tomorrow night, your place again?"

Chris dropped his blue eyes to the floor. "I don't think it's a good idea, Jay." He looked up at his best friend, hoping he would understand why he needed a break.

Jason raised his eyebrows and then nodded. "All right, man. I'll cover for you," he said, patting Chris on the shoulder. "You sound like you have some stuff to deal with."

Chris smiled slightly and grabbed the top of his head. He tensely pulled on his short blond hair. "Thanks, guy," he replied, feeling not at all relieved.

CHAPTER 4

Sitting in his fourth period journalism class, Bryan paid no attention to his teacher. His brown eyes had drifted to the picture of Courtney that he kept in his wallet. Bryan had treated Courtney like the treasure she was, the whole time they had been together. What had he done wrong? As if breaking up with him wasn't hurtful enough, Courtney had made the situation much more painful by immediately dating one of his friends.

Bryan had liked Courtney for over a year before they began dating. *Chris knew that.* Bryan and Courtney had celebrated their year-and-a-half anniversary right before Courtney broke up with him. *Chris knew that, too.* Bryan had been Chris's friend for close to a decade. *How could Chris see nothing wrong with dating Courtney?* Bryan loved Courtney more than anyone. He hated himself for introducing her to one of his own best friends.

Bryan couldn't understand why Courtney was attracted to Chris. She was an ethical, devout Christian. *Shouldn't Chris look like Satan to someone like her?* Bryan realized that he had many flaws of his own, but Chris's flaws made Bryan's flaws look like virtues.

Courtney swore that Chris had nothing to do with their breakup. She said that ninth grade should be a year for new beginnings. She said she needed to grow up and, therefore, could not continue dating her middle-school boyfriend. Going to out-of-control parties, trashing people's homes, and experimenting with drugs did not register in Bryan's mind as "growing up." In fact, that was parallel to Bryan's life before he dated Courtney—a lifestyle he had been smart enough to abandon.

⊰✦⊱

That afternoon in the cafeteria, Courtney widened her eyes as she spotted Julianna Camen heading her way. She knew she would run into Julianna at some point that day, but she had hoped it wouldn't be in front of any of Chris's friends.

"Hi!" Julianna called out as she approached Courtney. "Where are we going to sit?"

"Hi," Courtney replied in an unfriendly tone. "I'm going to sit over there," she said and pointed to Chris's table. "If you need help finding a place to sit, I'm sure one of the teachers could assist you."

Julianna's eyes filled with pain as she stared at Courtney speechlessly. Courtney turned away from her, hoping Julianna wouldn't start crying or cause a scene.

"Do you know where Marielle is?" Julianna asked, referring to their other best friend. Courtney, Julianna, and Marielle had been a notorious trio since elementary school.

Courtney glanced around the cafeteria. "Hmmm… I invited her to sit with me," she answered slowly, "but I think she sat with Cathy Kagelli's twin sister."

"O-kay," Julianna replied gradually, sounding more confused than hurt by Courtney's deliberately mean response.

"I'll call you later," Courtney said dismissively before hustling across the room towards Chris.

After buying her lunch, Marielle Kayne walked over to Chantal Kagelli's nearly full lunch table. In homeroom, Chantal had wasted no time introducing herself to Marielle and making her feel comfortable.

"Hi," Marielle said as she approached Chantal. "Can I sit here?"

"Sure!" Chantal agreed with a warm smile.

"I was going to sit with my best friend Courtney," Marielle explained as she took a seat, "but I feel uncomfortable around her new friends."

"Courtney Angeletti?"

Marielle nodded.

"Don't let her friends intimidate you," Chantal remarked. "My sister is sitting there with her boyfriend Jason.

I thought of sitting there, too, but I can't associate with them anymore."

"Who's that Alyssa girl?" Marielle asked, referring to the blonde from their homeroom who was sitting at Courtney's table.

"Alyssa Kelly?" Chantal asked while raising her eyebrows. "She *was* my best friend until she stole my boyfriend. So, as you can guess, we're not close anymore."

"Who dumped *you* for *her*?" Marielle asked. Although Alyssa was pretty, Chantal was stunning.

Chantal scoffed. "Jon," she replied and pointed to an attractive boy sitting beside Alyssa. "Except that's not how it happened."

"What do you mean?" Marielle asked, feeling at ease with Chantal.

Chantal sighed. "It's a long story. I guess it's no secret, though. Pretty much everyone from Sterling and Montgomery Lake heard about it."

"Oh, sorry to pry. You don't have to tell me," Marielle said quickly, perceiving Chantal's hesitation.

"Oh, it's okay. I just feel bad talking about them," Chantal admitted. "I guess it's better for you to hear it from me than from anyone else. I can only imagine how people twist the story when they tell it." She paused for a second and cleared her throat. "Jon and I grew up together in church and eventually started dating. After we'd been going out for a while, I became friends with Alyssa. She and Jon had been best friends for years, so she was always around. By the time Jon and I had been together for about six months, Alyssa was my best friend. I had no idea she liked him, so I trusted her with everything. Meanwhile, Cathy kept prodding me to break up with Jon because she thought he was mistreating me. One day, while I was at the mall with Alyssa, I think Cathy pretended to be me and broke up with Jon."

Marielle dropped her jaw.

"When I got home, I called him," Chantal continued, "and he seemed really confused to hear from his 'ex-girlfriend.' I asked him what he was talking about, but he said he had to go call his new girlfriend — Alyssa!"

"What?!" Marielle exclaimed, widening her brown eyes.

"Alyssa tried to claim there was nothing between her and Jon, but I kept hearing rumors they were together. After a couple of months, Cathy confirmed that they were a couple after all. Then the strangest thing happened… Cathy became close with Alyssa."

"Why would your sister become friends with a girl who backstabbed you like that?"

"I have no idea, but it ruined our relationship. That's when I started to think she and Alyssa might have plotted the breakup behind my back."

"What a mess! Did you confront Cathy?"

Chantal glanced towards her sister's lunch table. "I never accused her of anything because I have no proof. I just have a gut feeling she had something to do with it. I never even heard Jon's side of the story. After he told me Alyssa was his new girlfriend, I completely shut him out. I was heartbroken."

"I'm sorry you went through all that," Marielle said sympathetically. She did not like what she was hearing about Courtney's new clique. She didn't like it at all.

Butterflies fluttered around Courtney's stomach as she took a seat at Chris's lunch table. Even though it was only the first day of school, it was no secret that his table was the "popular" table. She felt honored to be the girl at his side.

"Hi, guys," she greeted everyone in a friendly manner. "What's up?"

"Hi, Court," Chris responded and smiled slightly.

As Courtney made eye contact with Chris, she perceived an unfamiliar, sad look in his eyes.

"Hey, Court!" Jon called from across the table, pulling her attention away from Chris. "This is Alyssa," he said, referring to the pretty blonde sitting beside him.

"Hi!" Courtney exclaimed. "I'm Courtney, Chris's girlfriend."

"Right," Alyssa said while looking Courtney up and down. She turned to Cathy, who was sitting beside her, and whispered something in her ear.

A small laugh escaped from Cathy's mouth. Then she sent a hard-to-read smile in Courtney's direction.

"Your sister dates my brother," Alyssa stated matter-of-factly.

"John Kelly is your brother?" Courtney asked, recalling her older sister Day's long-term boyfriend.

Alyssa nodded.

Courtney grinned. "My sister told me he had a sister, but she never said more than that. Small world!"

Alyssa smiled and turned back towards Cathy.

"Hi, Courtney," a familiar voice called out, stealing her attention away from the girls.

"Hi," she replied, turning towards her ex-boyfriend. "How's it going, Bryan?"

"Not too bad," Bryan said. "Hi, Chris."

"Hey," Chris answered lifelessly from the other side of Courtney. "Have fun last night?"

Bryan glared at Chris. Courtney could not blame him. How could Bryan have fun at a party while watching her make out with Chris the entire time? Knowing how deeply Bryan cared for her, Courtney imagined that the event had felt more like an emotional torture chamber than a party. *Why would Chris ask that question?* Chris was a nice person, incapable of intentionally hurting anyone's feelings. Either it was a misunderstanding, or he had been too messed up to remember the party.

"Did you?" Bryan retorted.

Chris shrugged. "I don't know. Did I?" he asked and turned to face Courtney.

Courtney nodded. "Of course, you did! Why else would you have invited everyone back for tomorrow night?"

"Is that what you want?" Chris asked as a hesitant smile spread across his full lips.

Courtney looked at Chris blankly. "Why does it matter what I want? It's your house."

Chris smiled at his girlfriend. He appreciated that she failed to take advantage of his offer or his parentless household. He didn't want to throw another party or even go to one. In fact, he didn't even want to hang out with his friends any longer. They would just sink him lower, and Chris was already struggling to keep his head above water.

"I thought you said the party was off?" Jason called from the far end of the table.

"Off?" everyone else questioned Chris in unison.

Chris glanced at his friends. He realized that, sadly, the only reason they were all close was their common love of partying. His roots were much deeper with Jason, Jon, and Bryan, but the rest of his friendships were surface at best.

"Well, I don't know," he responded uneasily and looked down at the table. "Maybe it's… it's just better if… I don't want… I just have to call it off."

"What's with you lately?" Cathy asked. "You've been acting weird ever since you hooked up with Courtney. Did your girlfriend brainwash you or something?"

At the sound of Cathy's accusatory words, Chris saw Courtney turn bright red. He knew Cathy was likely hungover and surely sleep-deprived, but that statement was harsher than anything he expected her to say.

"Don't bring her into this!" Chris demanded and stood up from his seat. "I don't want to have the party. Maybe I'm sick of having my house trashed and my family mad at me? Can you comprehend that possibility?"

Ten pairs of shock-filled eyes stared back at him while Cathy appeared unmoved by his outburst. "Whatever," she said, peeling her eyes off Chris and placing them on Courtney. She smiled before saying, "Maybe you don't want a party, but Courtney might."

"Of course, she does," Alyssa concluded. "I can tell just by looking at her that she's no low life. Right, Court?"

"Right," Courtney agreed.

Chris turned to face Courtney, wondering why she had changed her tune so quickly.

Cathy beamed. "I told you she was just like us," she said loudly.

Alyssa nodded and smiled at Courtney.

"Listen up, guys. If Chris doesn't have a party tomorrow night, you can count on one at my place," Jason informed everyone. "My parents are going out of town, and they're leaving Matt in charge. Luke has already started throwing out invites. It should be a good time."

"You realize your brother is out of control, don't you?" Alyssa remarked. "He's going to invite everyone he sees. The entire school is going to show up at your house."

"My night won't be ruined if you stay home." Jason coughed twice and laughed.

Alyssa glared at Jason as he playfully winked at her. "Come on, Courtney," she said, while standing up from the table, "let's go dump our trays."

Courtney immediately stood up and joined Alyssa at the end of the table. She grinned, and Chris assumed she was thrilled that Alyssa was being friendly to her after Cathy had been so hot-and-cold. Cathy seemed to resent Chris and Courtney's relationship, likely because of her loyalty to Bryan. To further complicate the matter, Cathy was best friends with Chris's ex-girlfriend, Lisa Ankerman. The idea that Courtney and Cathy would ever become friends, despite how convenient that would be for Chris and Jason, seemed farfetched at best.

CHAPTER 5

After school, Courtney entered her home and greeted her mother in their industrial-size kitchen. "Hi, Susan," she said halfheartedly.

"Courtney! Hello," Mrs. Angeletti replied, glancing up from a business proposal to face her youngest daughter. "How was your big, first day of high school?"

"School's never fun," Courtney replied and took a seat at the breakfast nook near a plate of freshly baked cookies.

"Well, I'm glad your day was good," Mrs. Angeletti responded sarcastically. "Tonight, your father and I are attending a dinner party at the Taylors' house. I left their number on the refrigerator. Don't stay up too late, okay?"

"Yeah, sure," Courtney agreed. "I'm going over Alyssa Kelly's house tomorrow off the bus. Don't expect me home until Saturday."

"Just leave her phone number and address in your father's office," Mrs. Angeletti said and looked back down at her work.

"Well, I would, but I don't have her number or her address," Courtney remarked between bites of cookie. "Sorry."

"How do you expect me to reach you?" Mrs. Angeletti asked, again looking up from her proposal.

"You could *finally* buy me a cell phone," Courtney suggested. "I mean, I'm in high school now. Most kids in my grade have had phones since they were ten."

"Seriously, Courtney," Mrs. Angeletti scoffed and looked eye-to-eye with her. "Your father is the mayor. We are strict with you for a reason."

Courtney rolled her eyes. "Lucky me."

Mrs. Angeletti sighed. "I'm all for you making new friends, but I need to know where you're staying. It's time you and I become more like mother and daughter than friends."

"Susan," Courtney began in a patronizing tone, "I'd rather have a friend than a mother. You're doing a good job. Let's keep it that way. Okay?"

Mrs. Angeletti stared at Courtney through the sky-blue eyes Courtney had inherited. Although they had not spent any quality time together since their June trip to the Hamptons, Mrs. Angeletti had noticed something was different about her daughter. Courtney had always dressed casually, worn little makeup, and valued the simple things in life. Suddenly she seemed to have transformed into a little woman. Her hair now fell freely to her shoulders, escaping the bonds of her usual ponytail. Her Chapstick had been replaced by frosted lip-gloss. In place of her backpack was a designer leather tote bag. Instead of being laced into sneakers, her feet were now raised on three-inch platform heels. Mrs. Angeletti could easily pinpoint Courtney's physical changes, but she felt uneasy about her daughter's recent attitude adjustment. She wanted to write it off as typical fourteen-year-old behavior, but the change in Courtney was continuing to concern her.

"You're right," Mrs. Angeletti stated firmly. "Let's spend the rest of the day together. I can finish my work later. How about we go to the mall, and I *finally* buy you a phone?"

Courtney shrugged. "Fine, as long as Dad pays the bill."

After school, Marielle entered her contemporary home and greeted her golden retriever. "Hi, Angel," she said. "How was your day?" Not expecting an answer from her loyal pet, she strolled into the kitchen. While playing her voicemail, she searched through the refrigerator for something to eat. The only message was from her mother, informing her that she should start cooking dinner at four forty-five.

Thanks, Mom, Marielle thought. *You know how much I love to cook.*

Her phone began to ring as Marielle decided to make a sundae. After grabbing a pint of coffee ice cream from the freezer, she answered the call. "Hello?"

"Hi," a soft, unsteady voice responded. "What's up?"

"Hey, Julie!" Marielle cried. "Is something wrong?"

"*Very* wrong," Julianna sobbed. "My parents are splitting up."

"Since when?" Marielle asked as she began scooping ice cream into a large bowl. "That's horrible!"

"Tell me about it!" Julianna exclaimed. "It's the worst. They bought me a Dalmatian, as if it would make up for ruining my life."

"Oh, Julie," Marielle said sympathetically, "at least they got you a puppy. Just that shows they were thinking of you."

"Yeah," Julianna admitted reluctantly. "I just don't understand. I thought my parents were happy. This completely blindsided me, just like Courtney ditching me in school today. I never saw any of it coming. Maybe I'm just clueless?"

"Wait. What did Courtney do?" Marielle asked and set aside her ice cream.

"She refused to eat lunch with me and made sure to let me know she had invited you to sit with her," Julianna replied.

Marielle's heart sank. Julianna had been Courtney's best friend for ten years—even longer than Marielle. She knew Courtney had been acting a bit shallow, but she never expected her to deliberately hurt Julianna. To say Marielle was worried about Courtney was an understatement.

"I don't know what's wrong with her," Marielle said in an attempt to comfort Julianna. "I'm glad you sat with me and Chantal. I don't think we'd like Courtney's new friends, anyway."

Marielle and Julianna got into a long conversation about Courtney and divorce. Marielle's parents had separated a month after she was born, so she knew the pain of not having a father in her life. Marielle reminded Julianna that she was lucky to even know her dad and that the separation did not have to be permanent.

Angel suddenly began to bark, diverting Marielle's attention from Julianna. She glanced at the clock on the kitchen wall. Four fifty-five. "Oh, my gosh!" she exclaimed, hearing a car door shut outside. "Julie, I'm sorry but I have to go! I'll call you later if I can. Bye!"

After tossing her phone onto the counter, Marielle searched through her kitchen cabinets. She frantically selected a can of small shrimp, sliced potatoes, and diced tomatoes. After placing a pan filled with hot water on her electric cooktop, Marielle retrieved a box of ziti from the lazy Susan. When her mom entered the kitchen, she felt confident she appeared organized.

"Hi, Mom," she greeted her while glancing up from the stove. "Supper should be ready soon."

"Really?" Mrs. Kayne questioned her in a skeptical manner. "And how do you expect the water to boil if the stove is off?"

Marielle's eyes traveled to the cooktop. Indeed, the knob read OFF. "I'm such an idiot! How could I forget to turn on the stove?"

"Well, if you do things in a rush, you usually don't do them well, but... you *will* be a great cook someday."

"Thanks," Marielle replied and turned the knob to HI. "Oh, my gosh, I wanted to tell you! Mr. and Mrs. Camen are splitting up!"

"Julianna's parents? When did you hear that?"

"Julianna called me after school. She was hysterical," Marielle explained while adding a teaspoon of oil to the water.

"Marielle, did you forget? I'm sure it was important for you to speak with Julianna, but you're grounded from the phone."

"I still don't understand why!"

Mrs. Kayne scoffed. "Why? I gave you four-hundred dollars to buy school clothes, right?"

"Right."

"You bought more expensive clothes than I own! A Burberry peacoat?! Not to mention the black, tan, and brown UGG boots! Um, what else—"

"—I told you I got good deals!" Marielle interrupted her. "Don't even accuse me of shoplifting!"

"I'm not stupid. Courtney, bought you all that stuff with her parents' money," Mrs. Kayne said. "The money I gave you went as far as the jeans and sweaters."

"You know Courtney," Marielle whined, dramatically throwing her arms up in the air. "She bought everything I said I liked. When we got back to her house, she said, 'Oops! I must have grabbed the wrong sizes. Take them.'"

"Once again, Marielle, I'm not stupid!" her mother cried. "You must have known what she was doing."

"I didn't!" Marielle exclaimed and stomped her foot on the ceramic floor.

"Control yourself!" her mother yelled. "Do you want to get grounded for another week? You could have cracked the floor with that temper!"

"I hate you," Marielle stated coldly and then trudged through the house to her bedroom.

CHAPTER 6

After walking home from school, Chris decided to begin tackling his homework with what little energy he had left. He had come to the conclusion that throwing a party the night before school started was one of the dumbest decisions he had ever made. Although every ounce of him wanted to crawl in bed, he sat at his kitchen table and opened his Algebra book.

Chris's greatest role models had always been his older cousins Taylor, Jordan, and Marc. They were not only elite football talents, but also exceptional students. Chris knew it was time to buckle down, academically, if he wanted to follow in their footsteps. In high school, Taylor and Jordan had been heavily recruited by Division-I colleges. Continuing on the same trajectory, Marc was about to commit to Boston

College. Chris dreamed of attaining that level of success, and he was thankful to have Marc at Montgomery Lake High to serve as his mentor.

Truthfully, Chris had grown up with little support at home. His parents had hired a live-in nanny to care for him and Katie throughout their childhood. As owners of an international consulting firm, his parents traveled to Europe on a regular basis. Once Taylor turned eighteen, Mr. and Mrs. Dunkin parted ways with their nanny and left Taylor in charge of their home whenever they traveled abroad. As Montgomery's hometown hero, Taylor could do no wrong in their eyes. Little did they know, their house would soon become Montgomery's hot spot for high school and college parties, turning their son into "the life of the party." Jordan eventually took over as house sitter until he left for college and passed the reins to Marc. Now that Chris was in high school, his parents had decided he was mature enough to babysit Katie and look after their home. For brilliant business owners, they clearly lacked sound judgement.

"You are such a loser," Katie stated crossly as she entered the kitchen, stealing Chris's attention away from his troubling thoughts.

"I can't believe a sixth grader is shooting me down," Chris muttered before turning back to his homework.

"What are you even doing?" Katie asked in a voice full of attitude.

Chris glanced over at her. She was peering at him with her hands on her hips. "I'm doing my homework," he replied.

Katie widened her eyes. "Are you sober?"

"Yes!" Chris exclaimed in an annoyed tone, although he knew her question was valid. "Yes, Katie, I am sober and trying to finish my math homework."

"That's a first," Katie retorted. "What time are your friends coming over?"

Chris slammed his book shut. "They're not," he said and leaned back in his chair. "No more parties. I promise."

"Really?" Katie asked, softening her expression.

Chris nodded. "You were right. I've been pretty terrible to you," he admitted. "But I promise, that's all going to change. From now on I'm going to focus on school and football. I have my future to think about, and I've been heading down the wrong road long enough."

Bryan stumbled listlessly into his house after school and rubbed his aching head. Without greeting his family, he climbed up the stairs and crawled to his bedroom. His phone rang as he entered the room. He didn't recognize the number and considered sending it to voicemail, but something in his gut told him to take the call. "Hello?" he mumbled into the phone.

"Hi!" a perky female voice responded. "What's up?"

"Who is this?" Bryan asked and fell back onto his bed. "Courtney?!" He sat up straight in recognition of her voice.

"Of course," Courtney replied. "What's up?"

"Hey!" Bryan cried, suddenly not noticing his headache. "What's up with you?"

"Well, my mom just bought me an iPhone, and I wanted to test it out," she explained. "My fingers absentmindedly dialed your number."

"I'm glad you called," Bryan admitted.

Courtney fell silent.

"Hello? Court?"

"Do you want me to call you?" Courtney questioned him hesitantly.

Bryan laughed. "Of course, I do."

"I better go," Courtney responded and hung up abruptly.

The dial tone that rang in Bryan's ear stung both his headache and his heart.

CHAPTER 7

Walking over to Alyssa on the second day of school, Courtney loudly called out, "What's up, girl?"

"Not much," Alyssa replied and began walking with Courtney through the crowded corridor. "Did you bring your bus note?"

"Got it right here," Courtney replied, fetching the note from her pocketbook. "Oh, and check out what my mom got me," she added, holding up her shiny black phone.

"That's sick!" Alyssa exclaimed. "Hey! Cathy!" she yelled down the hallway.

"Hi!" Cathy replied, after slamming her locker shut. "What's up?"

"Check out Court's new phone," Alyssa said when she reached Cathy's locker.

"Nice," Cathy replied and stole the phone out of Courtney's hand. "This is the one Jason has. The best selfie cam. You know you could get in trouble for using this in school, right?"

"Then give it back to me and maybe no one will notice," Courtney responded matter-of-factly.

"Sorry," Cathy apologized and handed the phone to Courtney. "Let's go to homeroom."

"Did either of you guys see Chris this morning?" Courtney asked as they ventured down the hallway.

"I did," Cathy replied in an uneasy tone. "He was with Jason, and they both seemed pretty tense. It was kind of weird to see. Jay's never serious, unless it has to do with schoolwork, and they definitely were not discussing that."

"I hope Jay's not mad at Chris for canceling his party," Courtney said.

"No way," Alyssa stated assuredly as they stopped in front of Courtney's homeroom. "Jay may be a thorn in the side to most of us, but he doesn't get mad easily. They've been best friends since Kindergarten. There's more to friendship than a stupid party."

"They've actually never been in a fight before," Cathy said, "so I'm kind of worried. I can't imagine what they were arguing about."

"Well, let me know when you find out," Courtney said before entering her homeroom.

⸎

Later that day, Alyssa and Courtney waltzed through the double doors that led to the high school's courtyard. It was eighty degrees, sunny, and way too nice of a day to eat lunch inside the cafeteria.

Alyssa sighed as she reached the table where their friends were gathered. "Who's in my seat?" she asked, peering expectantly at Jon.

"I am," Jon responded, warily eyeing his girlfriend. "That's because Cathy took mine."

"Only because Jason took mine!" Cathy exclaimed defensively. "You can sit there," she suggested, pointing to the only open seat.

"What about Court?" Alyssa asked, taking the seat between Bryan and Lisa Ankerman.

Courtney cringed at the sight of Lisa. She was Chris's ex-girlfriend, Cathy's closest friend, and the prettiest girl in their grade. Courtney had never found another female more intimidating.

"You can sit here, Court," Bryan offered, rising from his seat. "I'll go sit with Chantal and Andy."

"No, that's okay," Courtney responded hesitantly, wondering how the seats had been labeled. After all, no one at the table had ever eaten in the courtyard. Was there some sort of social protocol she was unaware of? "We can just share the seat," she added, while placing her hands on Bryan's shoulders.

"Okay," Bryan agreed as his eyes lit up. "Fine with me." He sat back down and motioned for Courtney to sit beside him.

Alyssa stood up and grabbed Courtney's arm before she could sit down. "Let's go buy lunch," she suggested and nodded towards the cafeteria. "Cathy, come with us."

"Thanks for including me," Cathy replied sarcastically. "I feel so privileged."

Courtney glanced at Cathy with a perplexed expression. She had never met anyone so hot-and-cold. Jason even appeared put off by Cathy's rude remark. He rolled his eyes and then smiled at Alyssa, who seemed unfazed by Cathy's attitude. *She must be used to it by now*, Courtney figured.

As Courtney turned to leave the table with Alyssa and Cathy, she suddenly noticed Chris's absence. "Hey, where's Chris?" she asked, glancing from Alyssa to Jason.

"He went to buy a drink," Jason replied. "You should just take his seat—permanently."

Courtney eyed Jason strangely, finding herself taken aback by his comment. It appeared Jason and Chris's argument had carried over from the morning. Jason had always been welcoming and kind to Courtney, so she was surprised to hear him speak negatively about anyone, let alone Chris. According to Chris, Jason was the closest thing he had to a brother.

Deciding not to respond to Jason's remark, Courtney left the table with Alyssa and Cathy. As she walked across the large courtyard toward the cafeteria, she lost herself in thought. Why hadn't Chris saved her a seat? She had hardly spoken with him since yesterday's lunch, and even then, he had seemed distant. She thought back to Jon's Fourth of July party and the very moment she had spotted Chris staring at her through the fire. She remembered thinking he looked cute, dressed nicely in a collared polo, khaki shorts, and a Patriots hat. It wasn't until Jason came over and introduced Chris that she felt any attraction towards him. When Bryan told her that Chris was the one everyone went to for *fun*, she had grown immediately interested in getting to know him. Chris had not even seemed surprised when she joined him by the water, as if they had telepathically planned their whole lives to sit there. She remembered how strange it had felt to feel so comfortable with someone whose voice she had never heard.

"Courtney!" a loud voice projected from the lunch line. "Courtney!"

"Is someone calling me?" Courtney asked, escaping from her contemplation. "Oh, Chris!" she cried, spotting him near the front of the line.

"Hi," Chris greeted her when she rushed to his side. "What's going on?"

"Nothing really," Courtney replied, deciding the lunch line was not the best place to bring up his argument with Jason. "What's up with you?"

"Nothing," Chris said and affectionately placed his hand on her shoulder. "So, you're going over Alyssa's today?"

Courtney nodded.

"That's what Cathy said."

"You're coming to Jay's tonight, right?"

"I don't think so," Chris replied while reaching for a bottle of water. "I want to talk to you about that, okay? Go get your lunch, and then we can walk around the school."

"Okay," Courtney agreed. "Wait for me when you get out of line."

⟡

Chris turned away from his girlfriend and progressed in the line. How was he going to explain why he wasn't going to Jason's party without getting her mad? Chris did not expect her to understand because she had no idea what Jason's parties were like. Jason had two older brothers, and one of them — Luke — was even wilder than Jason. His oldest brother Matt was much tamer, but as the captain of the Varsity football team, Matt had plenty of friends who partied hard. The Courtney whom Chris had first met would have been able to take care of herself at a Davids' party. Chris was not so sure about this "new" Courtney.

⁎

Courtney selected a dark green lunch tray and then quickly joined Alyssa and Cathy in line. "Sorry that took so long. Chris said he wants to talk to me."

"About him and Jay?" Alyssa asked, abruptly turning away from Cathy to face Courtney.

"No," Courtney shook her head, "about his party."

"What about it?" Alyssa asked.

"I don't think he's going," Courtney replied.

"Don't worry too much," Alyssa comforted her. "I know Chris has been acting weird lately, but he'll show up. He'll probably be half-baked by the time he gets to Jay's, but at least he'll be himself."

"Maybe he's going to dump me!" Courtney exclaimed.

"I'm sure that's not it at all," Cathy spoke up while eyeing Courtney strangely. "What reason would he have to dump you?"

Courtney shrugged. "Do you think he found out about Bryan?"

"Found out *what* about Bryan?" Alyssa and Cathy questioned her in unison.

"No, that can't be it," Courtney said distractedly. She was the only one who knew she had called him.

"Maybe he has to stay home and babysit Katie?" Cathy suggested.

"Probably," Alyssa agreed. "If it will make you feel better, we can come with you for your talk with Chris."

"Would you?" Courtney asked while reaching for a bottle of water. "That would be great."

As the girls walked towards Chris a few minutes later with their lunch trays in hand, Courtney observed a worried look plastered across his face. "He's going to dump me," she whispered tensely to Alyssa and Cathy.

"No, he's not! Just talk to him," Alyssa said and pushed Courtney into Chris.

"I thought we were going to talk?" Chris questioned her and then glanced at the other girls.

"Whatever you say to me, they can hear," Courtney replied. The butterflies in her stomach were killing her patience. "What's wrong?"

"I wish we had some privacy," Chris said quietly and eyed Courtney intently.

"They're staying," Courtney insisted. "Why aren't you going to Jay's tonight?"

Chris sighed. "Look, Court, this is going to sound crazy, but I'm just sick of parties," he said and turned away from her. "Maybe if it wasn't at Jason's, I'd go."

"What's up with you guys?" Courtney asked and turned Chris around to face her.

"Nothing," Chris replied, dropping his eyes to the ground. "I just don't want to go to another party. I'd rather you not go either."

Courtney scoffed. "I can't believe you just said that! You can't boss me around! I'm going to Jay's party tonight with Alyssa. That plan has already been made."

"Courtney—"

"—I never would have gone out with you if I'd known you'd be like this!" Courtney interrupted him.

"No, Court, listen to me," Chris pleaded. "I really don't want you to go to Jay's. If you go, I can guarantee you will get in trouble. The Davids' parties get out of control."

Courtney lowered her eyebrows and glared at her boyfriend. She felt like she was talking to Bryan. Bryan had always tried to keep her away from his friends. Bryan had always tried to protect her from getting in trouble. That was what she could not stand about him! She hated being sheltered. Bryan had always said, "My friends are no good," and expected her to just accept that. Courtney wanted to use her own judgment and make her own decisions.

"Lay off, Chris," Alyssa spoke up from behind Courtney. "She'll be fine at Jay's."

"Just shut up!" Chris exclaimed and rolled his eyes. "This has nothing to do with you."

"That was real nice," Courtney stated sarcastically. "Have a nice lunch," she added and quickly pushed past her frustrated boyfriend.

Chapter 8

After school, Marielle clutched her phone tightly. "I don't think so," she said sadly. "My mom almost grounded me for another week yesterday, and I'm not even supposed to be on the phone. Chantal, I can nearly guarantee the answer will be no."

"Are you sure? Can't you just ask?"

"Oh, no!" Marielle exclaimed. "Then she'll know I was on the phone after school. I really wish I could sleep over though."

"Just tell her I asked you in school," Chantal suggested enthusiastically. "It's the truth."

"I'll try," Marielle agreed and cleared Chantal's number from her call log. "But don't expect me unless I call. My mom should be home any minute, so I better go."

"Hope to hear from you," Chantal sang. "Bye."

"Bye," Marielle replied. She hoped by some miracle her mother would allow her to go to Chantal's house because she really wanted a new friend. She felt as if she hadn't spoken with Courtney in years, and Julianna was too preoccupied with her family issues to be any fun. In school, Marielle and Chantal had clicked immediately. There was something different about Chantal, something genuine. Somehow Marielle felt more comfortable with her than her own best friends.

⸻⸻❈⸻⸻

"I don't see why you didn't dump Chris," Alyssa stated as she and Courtney stepped off the bus. "He was kind of a jerk to you today."

"To you, too," Courtney agreed, observing the houses that lined Alyssa's development. They were all Victorian homes, but none were as large as the Angelettis' mansion.

"Yeah, well, I'm kind of used to it by now," Alyssa said. "Chris and Jason aren't the nicest guys to hang out with. I still don't get why everyone makes such a big deal out of them."

"Well, Chris is entitled to his own opinion," Courtney mumbled and looked down at her feet.

"He obviously doesn't think I'm entitled to mine!" Alyssa laughed.

"I think guys are just hypocrites," Courtney replied, shrugging helplessly. She glanced up at Alyssa, surprised to see her lighting a cigarette. Courtney knew that Chris and some of his friends smoked, but Alyssa seemed way too clean-cut for the habit.

"Here," Alyssa said and offered Courtney her cigarette. "You smoke, don't you?"

"Well... sometimes," Courtney lied and hesitantly took the cigarette from her friend. She hoped she did not look as intimidated as she felt. Why would Alyssa assume she smoked? She had never smoked anything in her life!

"I thought Chris said you did," Alyssa added, peering at Courtney expectantly.

"I'm usually trying to get him to quit," Courtney replied, nervously holding the cigarette between her fingers. Did all of her new friends smoke? Would she have to pretend to smoke to meet their standards? Why would Chris lie? Was he embarrassed by her morals?

"Then someone's a hypocrite," Alyssa teased her as she reluctantly took a drag off the cigarette.

Courtney laughed as she exhaled, trying to hide how disgusted she was by the lingering taste in her mouth and her own weak behavior.

"Chris was the first one of our friends to smoke; good luck trying to get him to quit," Alyssa said. "Jon and Jason have been giving him crap about it for years. He doesn't care that his two best friends think it's disgusting."

"It's always worth a try. I almost got Bryan to quit when we were dating. He gave up everything else," Courtney said, hoping Alyssa would take back her cigarette. The last thing she wanted was for anyone to see her holding it. She was the mayor's fourteen-year-old daughter!

"I haven't seen Bryan smoke in a long time," Alyssa commented. "He rarely did it to begin with. I'm pretty sure you got him to quit."

Courtney shrugged. "Maybe. I don't really see him much anymore. How long of a walk do we have to your house?" she asked, peering ahead at the line of large homes. She suddenly felt overwhelmed with anxiety.

Alyssa shrugged. "Another few minutes or so. My parents aren't home, so don't worry about smelling like smoke. Are you nervous about Jay's party?"

Courtney shook her head and quickly handed the cigarette back to Alyssa. "I would be if I wasn't going with you. Jay is more of Chris's friend than mine, and I don't even think they're on speaking terms."

"Yeah, but everyone likes you," Alyssa stressed before taking a drag of her cigarette. "Knowing Jay, he invited you because he wants you," she added. "Seriously, he must have asked me five times today if you were coming!"

"Really?" Courtney asked. "He wants me even though he's with Cathy?"

"Jay just wants someone to hit on in case he gets in a fight with Cathy tonight," Alyssa clarified and tossed her hardly smoked cigarette to the ground.

"Well, I know Bryan will be there, so that should make my night interesting," Courtney said quietly.

"Oh, Courtney, you still like him!" Alyssa sang with widening eyes. "Don't even try to deny it. Do you realize your face lights up when you hear his name?"

Courtney blushed. "Stop!"

"I knew it!" Alyssa exclaimed. "This is so perfect! Bryan will be there, and Chris won't. Maybe you guys can talk and work things out. Maybe you'll both get drunk and then when…"

Perhaps it is best that Chris isn't going to the party, Courtney thought. *Bryan will be there, and maybe it will give me a chance to figure things out with him.* In the meantime, she needed to figure some things out for herself.

What world was she stepping into? What was she welcoming into her life? Saying no to drugs had always been easy for Courtney. Why hadn't she been able to tell Alyssa that she didn't smoke? Was she seriously becoming that weak of a person? Why did she feel the need to fit in to the point of rejecting her own morality?

Courtney thought back to Chris's party, remembering how strange Chris and Jason had acted. She had never seen intoxicated people act that way. Honestly, she suspected they had been on some sort of hallucinogenic. Asking Chris was pointless; she knew he couldn't remember anything from that night.

Courtney had hoped to rub off on Chris, as she had on Bryan. Now, she was beginning to wonder if she was the one being influenced. Were Chris and his friends rubbing off on her? A small voice inside of her caught her attention. "Bad company corrupts good morals," it spoke. That was the voice Courtney had been drowning out for weeks, even though she knew it was the Voice of Truth.

CHAPTER 9

Hours later, Alyssa and Courtney began walking to Jason's party through the thick summer night's air. The sweat raining down Courtney's neck was a result of not only the heat index, but also her anxiety. Suddenly, she felt awkward going to the party. As her eyes traveled down to the low cut of her tank top, she wished she had brought a sweater. Why was she feeling so condemned?

Courtney was trying to convince herself that everything would be all right, but Chris's warning was playing like a broken record through her mind. The sinking feeling that had settled in her stomach was causing her hands to tremble. If anything did go wrong, whom could she turn to? She had betrayed Chris and would not blame him if he never spoke to her again. Technically they were still a couple, but Courtney felt alone. She could not recall a time when she felt so insecure.

⁂

Inside the Kagellis' colonial home, Chantal greeted Marielle, "Hey! I was just about to go outside to wait for you. Here, let me help you with your stuff."

"Thanks," Marielle replied while handing Chantal her pillow. "Sorry if I'm early, but my mom figured she could drop me off on her way to the supermarket. I'm just so glad she let me come! Sometimes I think she is two different people."

"It's fine," Chantal laughed and led Marielle up a set of stairs.

"Where's your sister?" Marielle asked and followed Chantal to the top of the stairs.

"At a party," Chantal replied while turning down the hallway towards another flight of stairs.

"Your house is nice," Marielle remarked, proceeding up the stairs behind Chantal. "I think Courtney and your sister went to the same party. It was at Jason Davids' house, right?"

Chantal nodded. "Yeah, Cathy said something about Courtney getting ready with Alyssa. She sounded kind of jealous."

"A lot of people are jealous of Courtney," Marielle commented as she entered Chantal's large bedroom. "I've been best friends with her since third grade, and sometimes, I'm even jealous of her."

"I don't think Cathy is jealous of Courtney. I think she's just jealous of the way Alyssa is treating her," Chantal stated thoughtfully as she placed Marielle's pillow on her neatly made bed. "The girls in that group can be territorial."

"See, Courtney's not like that," Marielle said, dropping her bag to Chantal's hardwood floor. "I'm beginning to doubt how much she really fits in with her new clique. She, Julianna, and I always hung out. This week, she purposely made Julianna cry and did not call me once. She's been different ever since she started hanging out with Chris. What do his parties do to people?"

Chantal let out a short laugh. "Well, I went to a couple of parties at Chris's when I was going out with Jon," she said, sitting down on her plush bedroom couch. "One of them was really bad. Almost everyone went crazy rebellious, including my sister. She met Jason at that party and went downhill from there. Now she's practically an alcoholic and a burnout."

"She changed that much in one night?" Marielle asked.

"Oh, no! That party was in seventh grade," Chantal clarified.

"Oh, okay," Marielle said, letting out a sigh of relief. "So, what was the party like itself?" she pressed, hoping her curiosity would not annoy Chantal.

"I didn't stay long, but long enough to get in a fight with Jon," Chantal said and rolled her eyes. "Chris's cousin was passing around a blunt, and Jon took a hit—not to mention he was already buzzed. Jon had always claimed to be 'against drugs,' so his behavior upset me. I tried to tell him, but he wasn't interested in anything I had to say. After our fight, I felt uncomfortable, so Alyssa and I left the party."

"That was nice of her to leave with you," Marielle commented while glancing at the pictures lining Chantal's walls. Most of them were of Chantal and her boyfriend Andy Rosetti. There were a few of Jon and even some of Alyssa. "I'm sure she'll do the same for Courtney. They're becoming pretty close."

"Did you tell Courtney what I said about Alyssa?" Chantal asked, eyeing Marielle questioningly.

Marielle shook her head. "I decided to mind my own business."

"I felt really bad after I told you about what happened to me. I shouldn't have said anything to taint your perspective of Jon or Alyssa," Chantal admitted nervously.

"No. I really appreciate you telling me about Courtney's new friends," Marielle assured her. "I'm not exactly jealous of all the attention she's paying them, but I do miss her."

"Don't worry. She and Alyssa won't stay close for long," Chantal concluded sympathetically.

"Well, Courtney does seem happy," Marielle said, studying an old picture of Cathy and Chantal on Chantal's wicker nightstand. Marielle struggled to tell them apart because they both looked cheerful.

"When I was going out with Jon, Bryan was with Courtney, but he never brought her out with us," Chantal said. "What's she like?"

"In our middle school, all the girls wanted to be her friend, and all the guys wanted to date her. I always assumed it was because her father is the mayor," Marielle explained. "She never really felt the need to befriend everyone; she was happy just goofing around with Julianna and me. She spent a lot of time at her church or with Bryan. When she started dating Chris, her priorities changed. She became consumed with her looks and popularity, instead of going to church or being a good friend. I'm actually kind of worried about her."

"Maybe someday I'll get to know her, but not if she's friends with Alyssa," Chantal said. "Honestly, I have never resented anyone more in my life. It's awful. I should not hold resentment, and I know that. I just… I've never been so hurt. Jon was my love, you know? I know I still love him. I'm pretty sure I always will. I feel so bad talking about them, but I just don't want to see Courtney fall into the trap I did."

"I know. I know you're just trying to look out for her. What's Alyssa like anyway?" Marielle asked.

"She's different now than she used to be," Chantal said quickly. "I'm probably not the best person to ask because of the bad feelings I have towards her. She used to be awesome: fun, friendly, and loyal. I don't know what happened. Bad company corrupts good morals. That's for sure. She's gotten into most of the stuff the rest of her crew is into. The stuff they do is messed up."

"Courtney doesn't sound like them at all," Marielle stated, shaking her head.

"It's actually really sad because most of those kids are really nice people. In sobriety, Jason and Chris are awesome. Jason's *brilliant,* although he's been making a lot of dumb decisions lately. Chris is probably the nicest guy I know. Bryan's a sweetheart, too. I don't think Bryan's as bad as the rest of them. I honestly don't know anything about Jon anymore. I pray for him all the time. I don't understand how he can be comfortable surrounding himself with darkness. He was raised as a Christian. I know he loves God. I never expected him to turn his back on his faith and become consumed with partying. I can't even talk about it, or I will get upset."

"What girls do they hang out with besides Alyssa and Cathy?" Marielle asked, trying to shift the conversation away from Jon for Chantal's sake.

"Oh, Lisa Ankerman and Leslie Lucus," Chantal replied, pointing to their pictures on her wall.

"Isn't your boyfriend friends with them?" Marielle asked as she recalled seeing both girls at Andy's locker.

Chantal nodded. "Yeah. Lisa is Andy's childhood best friend. They're like brother and sister. Lisa and Leslie date Andy's friends, Jeff and Adam."

"But their girlfriends hang out with Cathy instead of you? That's surprising," Marielle commented, lowering her eyebrows in confusion.

"After Jon and I broke up, I chose to shy away from his friends. It gets lonely, but I pray daily for strength not to compromise my beliefs. I have no interest in partying, and that's all they do now."

Marielle was still perplexed. "How are Lisa and Leslie even connected to Jon and Cathy if they're in Andy's clique? I can tell just from two days of eating lunch with you and Andy that his friends are not partiers."

Chantal laughed. "No, they're definitely not partiers, but Lisa is Cathy's best friend. She used to date Chris. They really loved each other, but Chris was in a bad place a few months ago. He broke up with her because he didn't want to bring her down with him."

"Oh, so, she probably *hates* Courtney!" Marielle cried with wide eyes.

Chantal shrugged. "I'm not sure, but things are weird now that Lisa and Chris have both moved on to other people. Lisa hangs out more with Andy's friends now. She's still friends with Cathy, Alyssa, Jay, and everyone, but it's awkward because of her history with Chris."

"Chris isn't afraid of bringing Courtney down?" Marielle asked.

Chantal bit her bottom lip and eyed Marielle warily. "Chris is in a better place now than he was then," she said after a few seconds of hesitation. "I'm sure he would break up with Courtney if he… uh… I shouldn't say. I don't want to gossip."

"It's okay. You don't have to tell me what was wrong with him," Marielle said, although her mind was racing with possibilities.

"Sorry… I'm not trying to get you worried. Chris is a really nice kid. He would never let himself bring Courtney down. Trust me."

"I hope not."

"The fact that he's going out with someone straightedge tells me he's trying to straighten out," Chantal added and smiled slightly.

"Or he could just like the clout of dating the mayor's daughter," Marielle stated matter-of-factly.

Chantal shook her head. "Chris doesn't care about clout. I'm not close with him anymore because he's Jon's best friend, but he's still one of my favorite people."

"That makes me feel a little better," Marielle admitted.

"You probably think Cathy is the center of that group, but she met them through me," Chantal said, taking Marielle by surprise. "In seventh grade, they were *my* best friends. I pulled Cathy into the group."

"Breaking away from them must have been hard," Marielle assumed, admiring Chantal's ability to stay true to her morals.

Chantal nodded. "I miss my friends. I really do, but they're caught up in things I don't want to be around. Andy and my mom are the only people I'm close with now. After being betrayed by your best friend and your boyfriend, it's hard to trust anyone. I believe God will bring the right people into my life and give me the discernment to stay away from people who could lead me astray. He has a plan, and knowing that is enough for me."

The way Chantal spoke of God reminded Marielle of things Courtney used to say before she met Chris. Marielle had not been raised with religion, so the idea of getting discernment from God was foreign to her. However, she could not deny that Courtney had been a much nicer person when faith was central to her life.

"I hope Courtney stays as strong in her faith as you have," Marielle remarked, while glancing again at the pictures on Chantal's wall. "I'd hate to see her follow in Jon's footsteps."

CHAPTER 10

Jason's home was nearly a two-mile walk from Alyssa's. The mansion rested high on a hill, and Courtney's muscles ached as she trucked up his driveway. The cars that lined his driveway obviously did not belong to her fourteen-year-old friends. There were going to be a lot more people at Jason's party than freshmen. They were people she would mean nothing to, and that intimidated her. Courtney's heart pounded hard against her chest as she and Alyssa climbed the cobblestone front steps.

An older teenager with a beer in his hand greeted the girls at the front door. "Jason, your friends are here," the boy called out loudly and nodded towards Courtney and Alyssa.

Jason entered the foyer and staggered towards the front door. "What's up, guys?"

"You're obviously buzzing," Alyssa stated while walking past Jason into his elegant, two-story foyer.

"Hey, Court!" Jason greeted her warmly, thrusting his arm around her and pulling her inside his home.

Courtney pulled away from his embrace. "Did Chris show up?" she asked eagerly.

"No. He made it clear he wouldn't be," Jason replied, dragging her into the kitchen where their friends were gathered.

"Hi, guys!" Courtney exclaimed brightly to Jon, Cathy, Lisa, Jeff, and Leslie.

"Hey, Court!" Jon cried in a friendly tone. "Where's your man?"

Courtney shrugged. "I guess he's not coming out tonight. Is Bryan here?" she asked, hoping no one took her response out of context.

"Well, you see Court-ney," Jason sang, once again placing his arm around her shoulders, "I had some herb and a pipe. Jon, Bryguy, and a few others came over after school, so we pregamed up in my room. Some of my guests have brought more weed, but my pipe and papers are upstairs."

"So, Bryan went to get them?" Courtney assumed, observing the puffiness beneath Jason's glassy, blue eyes.

Courtney turned and studied Jon. He showed no sign of being high or drunk. She remembered Chris saying that Jon was straightedge, so she found Jason's words hard to believe. Jon seemed like a really good kid. He certainly stood out from the others.

The idea of Bryan smoking pot turned Courtney's stomach. She really expected him to be above that. Were

Jason's words purposely misleading or was Courtney just naïve?

"Do you want something to drink?" Jason asked while holding up a bottle of vodka.

"Uh, not right now," Courtney replied, edging herself away from Jason. "Not ever," she added beneath her breath.

Flee the evil desires of youth, and pursue righteousness, faith, love, and peace, along with those who call on the Lord out of a pure heart, a small voice inside of her spoke. Courtney's eyes began to fill up with tears as she became overwhelmed with conviction. What was she doing at a drug-infested party?

"Seeing that Chris isn't coming, I'm surprised you came," Cathy stated and eyed Courtney strangely.

"Why?" Courtney asked while fighting off tears. The coldness in Cathy's eyes added to Courtney's discomfort. It wasn't Courtney's fault that Jason kept hanging all over her!

"Hey!" Bryan exclaimed as he and Courtney collided. "Court, what's up?"

On instinct Courtney embraced him.

"What was that for?" Bryan asked while handing the pipe and papers to Jason.

Courtney looked into Bryan's matte eyes. She was not going to risk getting into a serious conversation with someone under the influence. Despite what Jason said, Bryan appeared perfectly sober.

"Who wants a hit?" Jason sang as he began rolling a joint with the papers Bryan had handed him.

"You know I'm all set with that crap," Bryan responded, grabbing Courtney's hand and pulling her closer into his arms.

Cathy pushed past Courtney, in a less than friendly manner, as she made way to Jason. Courtney did not give her the satisfaction of a glare in her direction. "What is wrong with that girl?" she whispered to Bryan.

Bryan shrugged and smiled. "Did Jay offer you a drink?" he asked while reaching into a nearly empty thirty-rack on the counter.

"Yeah, he did," Courtney replied, "but please don't drink tonight, Bry." She placed her left hand on Bryan's arm and looked pleadingly into his hazel-brown eyes.

"All right," Bryan agreed with ease. "What's going on?"

Courtney sighed and placed her head on Bryan's shoulder.

"Court, what's wrong?" Bryan asked, lifting her chin and searching her eyes.

I miss you. That's what's wrong! Courtney thought. *I had you and then I let you go. Therefore, I am overcome with self-pity. I hate how I am acting. I just want to leave this party and run back to my comfort zone.*

"What?" Bryan pressed, gently brushing a piece of jet-black hair from her flushed face.

"Do you think we could go somewhere and talk?" Courtney asked.

"Absolutely," Bryan said with a nod. "Hey, Jay?"

"Hey, what's up?" Jason replied, without glancing in Bryan's direction.

Bryan walked over to Jason with Courtney close behind him. "Can, uh, we go talk in your room?" he whispered.

Jason laughed loudly and glanced from Bryan to Courtney. "Yeah, dude. Help yourself! There are some condoms in the nightstand if you need one!"

Courtney dropped her jaw and widened her eyes in horror.

"Oh, shut up," Bryan demanded and pushed Jason hard in the shoulder.

Obnoxious giggles escaped from their friends, and numerous pairs of eyes darted from Courtney to Bryan.

"Yay!" Alyssa clapped, sending a mischievous smirk in Courtney's direction.

Courtney blushed deeply and followed Bryan out of the kitchen with her head down. The privacy they had requested was for nothing other than a serious heart-to-heart. Jason had made it unrealistically clear otherwise.

"They are so obnoxious," Courtney complained while tightly gripping the cherry railing and easing her way up the stairs.

"They're just playing," Bryan responded as they reached the grand, second-floor hallway. "They all like you a lot."

"I heard," Courtney replied flatly. "So, where's Jason's room?"

"Down this hall," Bryan said and nodded down the long hallway to the left of the staircase.

"I can't wait to breathe some fresh air," Courtney sighed, halting behind Bryan at Jason's door.

"You won't find it in here," Bryan said while opening the door to a strong odor of marijuana.

"This kid is ridiculous!" Courtney cried, shaking her head in disgust as she entered Jason's room. "Don't his parents suspect anything?"

Bryan laughed and shook his head. "Jay gets straight A's. His parents think he's perfect."

"Chris's room isn't even this bad," Courtney muttered.

"Do you want to talk somewhere else?"

"How much weed does this kid smoke?" Courtney rambled in amazement. "There is no way that he *alone* could have smoked all that today," she said pointing to a nearby ashtray with a few roaches in it.

Bryan sighed and climbed over the remains of Jason's pre-party.

"By the way—" Courtney sang nonchalantly.

"—No," Bryan interrupted her, turning her petite body around to face him.

"No, what?"

"Oh, don't even give me that!" Bryan exclaimed with a flirtatious smile.

He knows me too well, Courtney thought. "Well, I want to know… when was the last time you smoked?"

"Smoked what?"

"Anything!"

"You know I stopped smoking weed when I was with you," Bryan replied. "I may smoke a cigarette occasionally but not often. Why do you ask? Is it because I brought Jay his bowl?"

"Forget it," Courtney responded, regretting any tension she had caused. She knew Bryan would never lie to her. Bryan had never liked drugs to begin with. He had told her he only tried them because that was all his friends did for fun. She thought he had been joking when he said that was all they did. Now she understood exactly what he had meant.

"So, what's up for real, Court?" Bryan asked, sitting down on Jason's neatly made bed and pulling her down beside him.

"Oh, Bry, I don't want to ruin the party for you," Courtney sighed. "You should be downstairs getting trashed with your boys."

"Not when someone I care about is upset," Bryan responded without hesitation.

Courtney smiled, as tears began to glaze her eyes. "How much is that?"

Bryan groaned. "Why are you doing this? Why are you avoiding what you really want to talk about?"

"I'm not," Courtney said, shaking her head and leaning closer to Bryan. "I want to talk about us."

CHAPTER 11

<u>Chris Dunkin—9:00 p.m.</u>

Why am I sitting at home, on my living room sofa, with my little sister on a Friday night? My best friend is having a party. My girlfriend is there. Why the heck am I watching Nick at Nite? Is this the social level I have sunk to? I, "the life of the party" only two nights ago, am now a friendless, straightedge, low-life. What the heck?!

Why is the girl who inspired me to make something of myself now acting so dumb? I'm sitting here without her, miserably fighting the urge to crack open a beer or smoke a bowl. But why have I let drugs become such a large part of my life? My friends were stupid to follow my path. What scares me the most is that I know even Jason is a follower of my path. Jason, the kid with the worst reputation in my grade, is a follower of mine. Jason's reputation was given to the wrong person—thank God. I am just "the life of the party" and glad at that.

I am pathetic, but I will say, less pathetic than I was two nights ago. I'm going through Courtney withdrawal—but not the Courtney at Jason's party, the Courtney I met over the summer. Sure, she's still beautiful, but that's not important to me if she's going to start acting like my friends. I'm looking for so much more than that.

Both today and yesterday, I couldn't tear my eyes off this brunette in my science class. Before this year, I had never seen her or heard a thing about her. Her appearance is not exotically striking, but she is really cute. Her face continues to break through my thoughts of Courtney and that troubles me. Honestly, I'm finding myself less and less attracted to Courtney, but I feel responsible for her.

What am I going to do about her? She's at a party with a bunch of wasted guys, who are probably trying to take advantage of her, and I'm okay with sitting here, watching TV? No, definitely not.

In Chantal's bedroom, Marielle glanced up from the scrapbook she was perusing and said, "Tal, I think your phone is ringing."

"My gosh, I love this picture!" Chantal laughed, peeling her eyes off a seventh-grade snapshot of Jon, Chris, and Jason. "Hello?" she sang into her cordless phone.

"Hey, Chantal," a deep voice replied. "It's Chris."

Chantal dropped her jaw. "That's so weird! I was just looking at a picture of you."

"Really?" Chris asked. "Well, uh, why?"

"Just for laughs," Chantal stated. "My friend Marielle is sleeping over, and she wanted to see it."

"You should hang out with that girl more often."

"So, what's up?" Chantal asked, flipping to another page in her scrapbook. She pointed to a more recent picture of Chris. Marielle's eyes widened.

"Have you heard from Cathy at all?" Chris asked.

Chantal scoffed. "She would never call me."

"Have you heard from anyone at the party?"

"No. You're there, aren't you?"

"No, but Courtney is."

"Oh, my gosh, Chris! What happened?" Chantal asked with concern. Although she hadn't talked on the phone with Chris in over a year, she was not finding the conversation awkward at all.

Chris sighed. "We fought over Jason's party. I didn't want us to go, but she went anyway."

"Wait… *You* didn't want to go?"

"Honestly, Tal, I didn't."

"That's really good," Chantal commended him as her stomach fluttered. She had been praying for Chris on a regular basis for the past two years.

"I'm worried about Courtney, though," Chris confessed. "She is so innocent and naïve. The cops always show up at Jay's parties, and I know she's going to get in trouble. She didn't give me her cell phone number, Jay's house-phone is off the hook, he's not answering his cell phone, and I have no way of getting in touch with her. Have you or Marie heard from her?"

"Her name's *Marielle*," Chantal corrected him, "and I don't know Courtney. I used to see her at church, but we never met. She hasn't been there lately."

"Oh."

"But Marielle has been best friends with her for years," Chantal added. "I'm sure Courtney's told you all about her."

"Seriously?" Chris asked, sounding bewildered. "Can you put her on the phone?"

Back at Jason's party, Bryan stared intently at Courtney. "What?!" he cried.

"I'm going to break up with Chris," Courtney repeated. "I dumped you for him, and I regret it."

Bryan's heart began to race in his chest. "Wh-wh-why?" he stammered.

"Bry, I don't like him the way I like you," Courtney whined while running a hand through Bryan's thick brown hair. "You and I never fought once while we were together."

"True, but the breakup was pretty harsh, Court," Bryan retorted.

"Yeah, I realize that… I'm sorry," Courtney replied, biting her bottom lip. "If I were to break up with Chris, would you take me back?"

"Court, what are you about?" Bryan asked and rose from Jason's bed.

"I'm not 'about' anything," Courtney replied and stood up beside him. "I just want to apologize for hurting you so badly." She placed her hand over Bryan's pounding heart.

"Apology accepted," Bryan responded flatly while staring blankly ahead. He could not understand himself. He had been dreaming of a moment like this since their breakup. Why was he making it difficult for her?

"Bryan, look at me," Courtney pleaded and turned him around to face her. "You still have it in you, don't you? I mean, you said a half hour ago that you care for me. What were you getting at?"

Bryan sighed. "Court, I just don't know about you," he said, silently regretting his word choice. "I liked you so much, and you broke my heart because you decided I wasn't fun enough for you. Now you're about to break Chris's heart for whatever reason. Do you care about other people's feelings at all? I don't think I could put up with that kind of hurt again."

"Chris and I got in a fight!" Courtney cried. "He's depressed or something and not acting like himself. I mean, since when does Chris not want to socialize?"

"He's changing his ways for you," Bryan replied, "just like I did."

"But he's not talking to me about it!" Courtney exclaimed with tears glazing her eyes. "I don't want to hurt him, but I can no longer deny the feelings I still have for you."

"Chris and I are on poor terms as it is," Bryan commented and turned away from her.

"Then you know what, Bryan? Forget it!" Courtney raged and stormed out of Jason's bedroom.

"Court?" Bryan called, chasing after her. Since their breakup, he'd wanted nothing more than Courtney back in his arms. "Courtney, wait!"

Courtney halted at the top of the stairs with tears streaming down her face. Standing with her arms crossed, she kept her eyes locked on the floor.

"Court," Bryan whispered upon reaching her, "I'm sorry." Before she could turn away from him, he lifted her chin. Looking eye to eye with her, he began wiping away her tears. "I want our relationship back so bad. Please, let's go back to Jay's room and talk."

Courtney turned away from him.

"I'm sorry, Court," Bryan stressed, taking her hand. "Please let's talk. Please?"

Courtney looked up and gazed into Bryan's eyes. "Okay," she agreed softly and allowed him to lead her back to Jason's room.

At Chantal's house, Marielle was still on the phone with Chris. "So, you want me to call Court?" she inquired.

"I would love you if you called her," Chris replied. "Pleeeease," he begged.

"She'll probably get mad at me," Marielle stated flatly. "Couldn't you just call her? I mean, she's already mad at you."

"That was terrible!" Chris exclaimed playfully.

"Well, I want to help you, and I don't want Court getting in trouble. It's just that I don't want to get on worse terms with her," Marielle explained.

Chris sighed.

"Listen, if you really want me to call her, I will," Marielle agreed, less than enthusiastically.

"Seriously?"

"Yeah. You seem like you really care about her, and she deserves to know you're worried."

"Thanks, Marielle," Chris said. "You seem like a really good friend. It's weird that I don't know you. Honestly, I don't even remember Courtney mentioning you. Then again, I don't have the clearest memory. Do you know who I am?"

"Chantal and Courtney have both shown me pictures of you," Marielle replied, gazing at a collage on Chantal's wall, "and you're in one of my classes."

CHAPTER 12

Courtney stared intently at Bryan as they continued their conversation in Jason's bedroom. "Do you really mean that?" she asked in a tone filled with hope.

Bryan nodded and embraced her in his arms. "I want you back so badly. I'm sorry if I was a jerk a few minutes ago."

"It's okay. I'm just so glad you'd take me back," Courtney replied, hugging him tightly.

"I don't know how you're going to handle this with Chris, but I'm behind you all the way," Bryan pledged. "Having our relationship back is more important to me than anything."

"I'm so glad you feel that way. I do feel bad for Chris, though," Courtney admitted. "The thing is, I don't want to hurt him in the least bit. He's been nothing but nice to me. I was the one at fault in our fight. I should have listened to what he had to say and probably shouldn't have come here. I knew you would be here, so I really wanted to come. When I called you yesterday, I realized I liked you more than I could ever like Chris. I know I can't lead him on. I told you before that I was drawn to him, but I think I took it the wrong way. Maybe we were just meant to be good friends. Maybe he needed some encouragement."

"Just don't be harsh on him, okay?" Bryan requested. "Chris takes everything to heart."

"Maybe he's mad at me for coming here and wants me to break up with him?" Courtney contemplated. "It's just a thought, but maybe he will break up with me!"

Meanwhile at Chantal's, Marielle hung up the phone after calling Courtney's cell phone. "I can't get through," she said. "I hope everything's okay."

"Everything's fine. The music's probably so loud that she couldn't hear her phone," Chantal reasoned.

"That's a thought," Marielle agreed. "Sorry that I've spent most of the night on the phone."

"It's all right," Chantal said with a smile. "You're doing Chris a favor, and I think that's really nice."

"You said he's one of your favorite people. Why?" Marielle asked, once again glancing at his picture.

"He's cute, isn't he?" Chantal commented, following Marielle's eyes to his eighth-grade school picture.

Marielle nodded. "Yeah, Courtney's lucky."

"Chris is just really nice," Chantal began. "I'm sure you wouldn't guess from looking at him, but he's got a huge heart.

He's seriously someone you can't help but love. He can take anything and make it funny. I really miss hanging out with him.

"His parents go away a lot and leave him to look after his sister. Sometimes, they have his older cousins housesit, but that's how Chris got messed up in the first place. In the past year or so, he's gotten pretty deep into drugs—stuff beyond weed and alcohol. He sounded different on the phone tonight. You know, kind of like he used to before… well… you know. Seriously, Courtney is lucky to be with him. I really hope he stays on the track she's got him on."

"What track is that?"

"He just sounds like he has his head on straight again," Chantal replied. "Maybe Courtney's shined some light into his dark life."

Upstairs at the party, Courtney rose from Jason's bed. "We should probably head back downstairs," she said.

"Yeah," Bryan agreed and followed her, "before people start making up rumors about us."

"I think they already have," Courtney laughed. "I almost forgot there was a party going on downstairs. I can only imagine who else has shown up. Luke really did invite the whole school."

"Hopefully not any cops," Bryan said as he opened Jason's door.

"*That* would ruin things," Courtney commented while walking down the deserted hallway.

Bryan took Courtney's hand and led her down the stairs. She withdrew her hand from Bryan's before they entered the kitchen, where the party was still in full swing.

"Hey!" Jon greeted them, still appearing sober.

"Hi," Courtney and Bryan responded in unison.

"What have you two been up to?" Jason sang and patted Bryan's back.

"Oh, leave them alone," Jon interjected in an annoyed manner and walked over to Bryan and Courtney.

"What's up, bud?" Bryan asked.

"This party really sucks when you're the only one sober," Jon replied.

"Are they drunk or baked?" Courtney asked as she glanced over Jon's shoulder at Alyssa, Cathy, and the rest of the group.

Jon shrugged. "Does it matter? Alyssa is driving me crazy. Honestly, I don't even want to be here anymore. She was hanging all over me, so I was cool with that. Then she started drinking a beer, even though she knows I hate it when she drinks. The next thing I know, she's taking a haul of someone's cigarette, and that's not okay. I don't date girls who smoke, and I didn't think my girlfriend smoked! We've been together for over a year, and she's never smoked anything in front of me. So, after I avoided her for a half hour, she decided to take a hit off a joint Jay passed around."

"I saw her smoke earlier today. She doesn't normally smoke?" Courtney asked.

At the sound of Courtney's words, Jon's face turned red with anger. "No," he said flatly.

"What's gotten into her?" Courtney asked, peering at Alyssa. She was laughing hysterically and twirling Leslie around like a ballerina.

"I'm done with her; that's for sure," Jon stated sternly.

"You're going to break it off?" Bryan asked while glancing from Jon to Alyssa.

"If she keeps this up? Yeah," Jon replied and nodded intently. "Absolutely."

"Jay, I think your house-phone is ringing," Lisa called from beside Cathy.

"It's off the hook," Jason replied. "Whose cell phone is ringing?"

"Mine!" Courtney squeaked, rushing towards her bag on the counter. "Oh, my gosh! I forgot all about my phone! Crap, what if my parents were trying to reach me? Hello?" she cried into the phone, blocking her other ear as she rushed out of the kitchen.

"Court?" Marielle responded.

"Ugh, I can't hear you. Wait a minute." Courtney rushed up Jason's stairs with Bryan and Jon. "Marielle?"

"Yeah, are you okay?"

"Kind of. Why, what's going on?"

"I'm at Chantal Kagelli's," Marielle replied, "and Chris called. He sounded kind of worried about you, so I said I'd give you a call. Where have you been? I've been calling since nine-thirty!"

"I didn't hear my phone," Courtney replied. "Bryan and I were upstairs talking, and I left my bag in the kitchen. What's up?"

"Chris just wanted to know if you were okay," Marielle replied. "You are, right?"

"Was he going to come get me?" Courtney asked while entering Jason's bedroom.

"He said something about his cousin Marc who has a truck. He seemed really worried about you."

Wow. I can't believe he still cares after I was so rude to him. "Hold on, Mar," Courtney said as she turned towards Bryan and Jon. "Do you guys want to get out of here?"

Bryan shrugged. "Whatever."

Jon widened his eyes and nodded intently.

"Marielle, do you think Chris would still come get me?"

"Probably."

"And Jon and Bryan?" Courtney added hesitantly.

"I can call him and ask if you want," Marielle offered.

"Okay, call me back," Courtney said, giving Jon and Bryan a thumbs-up sign.

<hr>

Marielle hung up with Courtney and turned towards Chantal. "She wants me to call Chris and ask him to go get her, Bryan, and Jon."

"Jon, too, huh? Figures he would be at the party. She can't call her own boyfriend?"

"I guess not. She's with Bryan, so maybe something happened between them and she feels guilty. I don't know. I wouldn't put anything past her at this point."

"Well, call Chris then!" Chantal exclaimed and threw her phonebook at Marielle.

"I can't call him!" Marielle cried. "He'll think I'm weird or something. He probably doesn't even remember who I am. You call him."

Chantal laughed. "His brain is not *that* fried. He's expecting your call. What is wrong with you?"

"Can you please call him?" Marielle asked. "Please?"

Chantal rolled her eyes. "My gosh, you're acting like you like him or something."

Marielle turned her back to Chantal.

"Oh, my gosh, you do!" Chantal said accusingly. "Look at me."

Marielle turned towards Chantal with a hesitant smile on her face. "I don't even know him."

"Then call him," Chantal smirked, gesturing towards the phone. "You shouldn't be scared."

"I'm phone shy," Marielle said, regretting her lame response.

"Yeah, okay."

Marielle sent a playful glare in Chantal's direction and then continued to search for Chris's number. "Is there any certain order these numbers are in?"

"My phonebook's in chronological order. Chris is towards the beginning."

"Zero-six-three-five," Marielle read off, picking up the telephone. She didn't hesitate to dial his number. After all, he was expecting her call.

CHAPTER 13

Chris sat by his kitchen phone, shredding a piece of paper with his restless hands. "What the heck!" he shouted, stomping his bare feet on the ceramic-tile floor.

"Are you okay?" Katie called to him from the living room.

"Yeah, sorry," Chris replied, resting his chin in his hands and rubbing his forehead.

Chris had the unshakable feeling that Marielle was the girl in his science class whom he had found attractive. While on the phone with her, he had grown intrigued. She seemed laidback, agreeable, and considerate. She agreed to help him out at the risk of upsetting Courtney. Would Courtney do Chris an inconveniencing favor? By going to Jason's party, she had already answered that question.

The ringing telephone awoke Chris from his contemplation. "Hello?" he called, answering the phone and walking outside onto his back porch. He took a seat on a lounge chair and pulled a cigarette out of his pocket.

"Hi, Chris?" Marielle replied.

"Yeah, it's me," Chris replied after lighting his second cigarette of the day. He was trying his best to quit smoking, but he had become somewhat dependent on the vice. He had first tried smoking at age ten, and by age twelve, he had begun smoking daily. After almost three years, how could he not expect to be addicted? Even though his group of friends considered smoking socially acceptable, Chris had decided it did not suit the lifestyle he desired to live. In order to succeed in his football career, he would need all the lung capacity he could get. His cousin Marc, who was a co-captain of the Varsity football team, had been pointing that out to Chris for years. Jon and Jason had repeatedly expressed similar concerns. Smoking was just another item on the long list of things Chris wished he had never tried.

"It's me, Marielle. I talked to Courtney, and she, um, wants you to pick up her and, um, Bryan and Jon," she informed him.

"Are you serious? Bryan and Jon?" Chris complained.

"That's what she said," Marielle replied. "Do you still want to get her?"

"Yeah, it will just be kind of awkward," Chris said slowly as an idea entered his mind.

"Why?" Marielle asked. "Bryan and Jon are your friends, aren't they?"

Chris sighed. "Yeah, but it's screwed up."

"Oh," Marielle answered quietly.

"Hey!" Chris exclaimed brightly. "Would you and Tal want to come for a ride?"

"To get Courtney?" Marielle questioned him with a twist of surprise in her tone.

"Yeah, would you?"

"Hold on," Marielle replied.

Chris's heart pounded as he waited for Marielle to discuss the situation with Chantal. He flicked his not-even-half-smoked cigarette over the railing and walked back into his house. Saving Courtney from getting in trouble suddenly seemed less important as Marielle began to dominate his mind. Now that he knew Courtney was safe, he wanted to find out if Marielle was the cute girl from his science class.

"Chris?" Chantal's sweet voice rang into his ear a moment later.

"Hey, Tal."

"What's going on?" she asked. "You want us to come with you to Jay's?"

"Could you please?"

"It's not too late, so my mom may let us come," Chantal replied. "Talk to Marielle while I go ask, okay?"

"Sure," Chris agreed with ease.

"Hey," Marielle spoke into the phone a second later.

"Hi," Chris greeted her. A smile spread across his lips at the sound of her voice. "So, I guess you might be coming with me, huh?"

"Yeah, if you want me to," Marielle replied. "I'm sure I could wait at Chantal's if the car will be too crowded."

"Don't be ridiculous!" Chris exclaimed. "I want you to come. I want to meet the person who's helped me so much tonight."

"That's cool," Marielle stated flatly. "So, you really like Courtney, huh?"

"That came out of nowhere," Chris responded, pondering his answer.

"Sorry, you just seem like you really care about her."

"Don't be sorry. I see where you're coming from," Chris said, hoping he hadn't made Marielle feel uncomfortable.

"I'm happy for her," Marielle said, sounding at ease. "She's lucky to have such a caring boyfriend. Whether she shows it or not, I'm sure she appreciates you."

Chris sighed, wondering if he should tell Marielle how he *really* felt about Courtney. He was afraid she'd think he was weird if she knew the truth. Seriously, why would he go through so much trouble if he didn't love Courtney? He knew he must love her in some way. She had been such an inspiration to him. How could he not be there for her?

"Chris?" Marielle called. "Hello?"

"Oh, sorry, Marielle," Chris apologized. "I thought my sister was calling me."

"That's okay. Chantal says it's okay for us to go with you. Maybe you should check and see if your cousin can still bring us."

"Yeah, okay. I'll call you back."

"Me or Chantal?"

"You."

At the party, Jon sat in the hallway outside of Jason's bedroom, deep in thought. He couldn't motivate himself to charge downstairs and break up with Alyssa. It wasn't that he loved her; it was more his own fear of another foolish breakup.

When Chantal was Jon's girlfriend, he couldn't get enough of her. She was his dream girl: kind, loving, honest, loyal, and friendly with a heart after God. The last message Chantal left him had said something along the lines of, "It seems like you should just be dating Alyssa. It's clear to everyone that you have feelings for each other. Don't even bother calling me back." It was cold and aloof—something he had never expected from her.

How had his thoughts swayed towards Chantal? Alyssa was his girlfriend and current problem. She was downstairs—drunk and high—acting like an idiot. But that wasn't the Alyssa Jon knew! Had he done something to upset her? Was she purposely trying to upset him? It seemed that way. Why had the last two years of his life been filled with so much confusion and drama?

Jason's bedroom door creaked open as Bryan and Courtney stepped into the hallway. Courtney pulled her hand from Bryan's grip when she noticed Jon. Refusing to meet Jon's eye, she proceeded down the hallway towards the stairs. It was clear that Courtney and Bryan still had feelings for each other. Although Chris was Jon's best friend, he felt Bryan was justified in trying to win back Courtney. Jon still couldn't believe Chris saw nothing wrong with dating her.

"Did you break up with her?" Bryan asked while staring anxiously at Jon.

Jon sighed and adjusted his baseball hat. "No," he said and glanced over the railing to the foyer below. "What's going on with you and Courtney?"

Bryan shrugged and looked down at the carpet.

"Did Marielle call back?" Jon questioned him, gripping the railing tightly as he trudged down the stairs.

"No," Bryan replied. "Dude, are you okay?"

Jon remained silent as he walked across the foyer. While angrily stomping into the kitchen, he shouted, "Alyssa! What the heck is your problem?"

The chant of the party fell silent. Heads turned, and eyes peered.

Alyssa turned to Jon as her glassy eyes filled with fear. "Jon?"

"Yeah, it's your boyfriend, letting you know you're an embarrassment!" Jon screamed.

Alyssa stared at him blankly.

"I've had it!" Jon continued, drawing more attention their way.

"Jon, what is wrong with you?" Alyssa asked quietly.

"We're through," Jon stated flatly while looking eye-to-eye with her. "You've changed into someone I could never have a steady relationship with. I feel like I don't even know who you are. To this day, Chantal means more to me than you ever could."

CHAPTER 14

Back at the Kagellis' house, a hot flash shot through Marielle's veins when Chantal's telephone rang.

"Marielle, it's for you," Chantal sang, tossing her the phone.

Marielle's hand shook as she placed the phone to her ear. "Hello?"

"Hey, it's me," Chris responded coolly. "What's up?"

"Nothing's down," Marielle replied, attempting to calm her nerves.

Chris laughed. "Well, that's good. So, what are you and Tal up to?"

"Nothing really," Marielle said. "We were going to watch a movie, but there's really no point if we'll be going out."

"Oh, yeah, what movie?"

"Sydney White."

"Was that your pick or Tal's?"

"Both of ours."

"Can't you guys just watch it when you get back to Chantal's?"

"I guess."

"Maybe we could all watch it at my house," Chris suggested.

"What are you getting at?"

"Just that I'd like your company," Chris replied nonchalantly.

Marielle froze. Was he flirting with her? "You actually like that movie?" she asked, trying to figure him out.

"And you," Chris answered matter-of-factly.

"What?!"

Chris laughed. "Don't sound so surprised. You seem like a pretty cool girl, and I like hanging out with cool people."

"O-kay," Marielle replied hesitantly, making eye contact with Chantal.

"What's he saying?" Chantal whispered.

"So, you want to watch the movie with us?" Marielle questioned him.

"Yeah," Chris replied immediately.

"With Courtney, Bryan, and Jon, too?" Marielle asked in confusion.

"If they want," Chris said as though the idea had never entered his mind.

"Can I ask you a question?"

"Yeah, go ahead."

"Well, do you, like, still, um, I don't know," Marielle stammered while glancing again at Chris's school picture on Chantal's wall.

"You can ask me anything. I'm an open book."

"Well, are you and Courtney apart or something?" Marielle blurted out, hoping Chris was expecting that question.

"We're in a fight," Chris responded, "but I don't think we'll need to make up."

"What do you mean?"

"Uh, I don't know," Chris stammered. "I don't think we'll be together for long, I guess."

Marielle dropped her jaw. "But you're so worried about her! Don't you still like her?"

"Uh, not really," Chris admitted, "and I think she feels the same way about me."

"Really?" Marielle asked in disbelief. "Then why do you want to save her from the party?"

Chris sighed. "Don't get me wrong, but I have my reasons." He stared blankly ahead, considering how to tell Marielle the truth. He was intrigued by Marielle, and that was why he still wanted to pick up Courtney—but how had that transpired? Originally, Courtney had been on his mind. Then, after talking with Marielle, Courtney had merely become an excuse for conversation. What if he was wrong about Marielle? What if she was not the girl from his science class? Would that alter his opinion of her?

"Chris?" Marielle asked, sounding more confused than ever.

"Hi," Chris replied distractedly.

"Did I say something wrong?"

"No!" Chris stressed, escaping his daze. "You've been great. I was just thinking about what you said. You know, about why I'm going through all this trouble for Courtney."

"Yeah?"

"We just really need to talk things out. We've only been together for a month or two, and I don't think either of us will be heartbroken if we're not together tomorrow."

"So, you're going to break up with her?"

"I'm going to talk to her," Chris replied, "and yeah, probably break it off," he added. "I know you and Court are tight, but could you please not—"

"—Don't sweat it, Chris," Marielle interrupted him. "I won't say a thing. Considering the way she's acting, I think you're too good for her."

"Really?" Chris asked, thrown off by her unexpected words.

"So, what did your cousin say?"

"Yeah, he'll pick us up," Chris replied while dwelling on her last comment. If Marielle meant what she said, she obviously thought highly of him. Perhaps she was just as intrigued by him as he was by her.

Back in Jason's kitchen, Courtney stood silently beside Bryan and locked her gaze on Jon. It seemed as though everyone's eyes were planted on him, but Courtney's stared deeper. She knew inebriated people often raged, but Jon was completely sober!

A single tear streaked from Alyssa's right eye, but no one crept from their spots to comfort her. Jon didn't have to ream Alyssa out publicly. There were hundreds of other ways he could have broken off their relationship. Why had he gone out of his way to hurt her? What had she done to deserve such mortification?

Alyssa's tearful eyes drifted to Cathy. Courtney assumed she was seeking a sign of compassion from her friend. Cathy wrenched her eyes off Alyssa and glanced at the floor. Courtney watched Alyssa's pain-filled expression intensify as she stared disappointedly at Cathy. Alyssa's eyes began traveling from person to person, in search of comfort. Lisa, Leslie, and the other girls had their eyes pasted to the floor. Bryan's eyes were locked on Jon. He appeared disturbed by Jon's outburst. A short laugh escaped from Jason's mouth, and Courtney couldn't tell if he was amused or nervous.

"This isn't right," Courtney whispered to Bryan as she pushed past him towards Alyssa.

Bryan tried to pull Courtney back, but she pressed forward.

"Alyssa!" Courtney called, while moving between Alyssa and Jon.

Alyssa stared helplessly at Courtney. Her face was glazed with confusion and disgrace. All the eyes in the room immediately locked on Courtney.

"%$&^! The cops are here!" Jason's brother Luke yelled as he ran into the kitchen.

"Crap!" Jason exclaimed and turned his attention to the more serious dilemma. "Everyone, get out of my house!"

All eyes were torn off Courtney as chaos erupted throughout the party. The pounding on the front door was barely heard over the uproar of people scrambling towards alternate exits.

"Courtney!" Bryan hollered as he pushed towards her frozen body. "Court!" Upon reaching her, he grabbed her hand and pulled her through the crowd and into the foyer.

"What are we doing?" she asked in panic. "We have to get out of here!"

"Just follow me. I know what to do," Bryan said while opening a closet door. "Get inside."

"Are you crazy?!" Courtney exclaimed, halting at the door.

"They're going to rush in and check the rooms first," Bryan said, pulling her into the closet. "Just be quiet and hide. I know it sounds stupid, but it's worked before."

"Okay," Courtney agreed and began layering various coats on top of her. "What if my phone rings?"

"Shut it off," Bryan replied, continuing to layer coats and belongings on himself and Courtney.

"I can't see in here," Courtney whispered, searching desperately through her pocketbook.

"Shhh," Bryan hushed, hearing the front door squeak open.

"Police!" an officer shouted and charged into the foyer. From above Courtney's head, she heard the stomping of policemen climbing the set of stairs. Blood rushed through her veins, and the hairs on the back of her neck rose. Her eyes widened with fear as an officer paused outside the closet door.

Bryan gripped Courtney's hand tightly and pulled her deeper into the walk-in closet. The closet extended completely beneath the set of stairs, forming an L-shaped passageway. "I can't see any better than you can but try to pull as many boxes and big things in front of you as possible," Bryan whispered nervously.

Courtney crawled deeper into the closet with the coats still layered upon her back. The ceiling arched lower as she and Bryan made a sharp right near the end of the closet. Courtney's heart pounded hard against her chest. After crawling as deeply below the stairs as possible, Bryan and Courtney fell flat on their stomachs. Courtney's heartbeat seemed to vibrate on the cold tile floor as she adjusted the coats to cover her petite figure. "They're going to search in here and find us," Courtney trembled.

"No, they're not," Bryan hushed. "Did you see how many people ran upstairs? Did you notice the crowds in the other rooms?"

"Yeah, I guess," Courtney answered faintly.

"Yeah, and there are a lot of drugs and alcohol in the kitchen. The cops are going to be busy," Bryan added.

"I hope you're right," Courtney said, wishing she had heeded Chris's warning. Chris had proven himself right, and Courtney felt like more of a jerk than ever. She had irrationally flipped out on him, yet he was still trying to help her escape from this hellhole. Clearly, Chris did not have a malicious bone in his well-built body.

Chapter 15

Chantal smiled as she opened her front door. "Hi," she said, welcoming Chris and his older cousin into her home.

"Hey," Chris replied distractedly while looking around the foyer. "Where's, uh, Marielle?"

Chantal lowered her eyebrows and glanced at him suspiciously. "She's fixing her hair," she replied.

"I'm Marc," Chris's cousin introduced himself and set his light blue eyes upon Chantal.

"I'm Chantal, but you probably knew that already," Chantal replied and shook his hand.

Chantal had been hearing good things about Marc Dunkin for years, first from Jon and then from Cathy. Jon thought Marc was a good influence on Chris; Cathy thought Marc was gorgeous—she wasn't wrong. His eyes might have been a half shade lighter, but they were large and round just like Chris's. Also, like Chris, Marc had warm blond hair, trimmed short and spiked up. He was well-built and most likely a great athlete like his younger cousin.

"So, Chris's chic is your friend?" Marc implied with a crooked smile.

"Not really. She's more of Marielle's friend," Chantal replied.

"Ah, the girl Chris is into," Marc stated, seeming amused by the situation.

At that moment Marielle paused on the step she had been descending. A bewildered expression coated her face as she glanced from Chris to Marc. She continued to walk down the stairs, slowly and stiffly.

"Yeah, that's right," Chris spoke with his eyes fixed on Marielle.

Chantal's eyes traveled from Marielle to Chris and then to Marc. "Did I miss something?" she asked quietly, struggling to tear her eyes off Marc's attractive face.

"I tried calling Courtney again," Marielle stated, "but there was still no answer. I don't know what to make of it because she was expecting my call. I hope everything's all right."

"Hey, Marielle," Chris said while looking her up and down. "I, uh, do recognize you from Biology."

"Cool," Marielle replied, sending a warm smile in his direction. "I, um, recognize you, too."

"We should probably head over to the party before the cops show up," Marc suggested, jiggling his keys.

"Yeah, 'cause they always do," Chris agreed and turned from Marielle to face his cousin.

"Last I heard it was pretty rowdy over there," Marc added. "A lot of my friends are there."

"I hope the cops aren't!" Marielle exclaimed with wide eyes. "Maybe that's why Courtney's not answering her phone? Maybe she got arrested?"

"No," Chris shook his head, placing a comforting hand on Marielle's shoulder. "She's smarter than that. Plus, she's with Jon and Bryan. They both know how to outsmart the cops at Jason's house."

Marielle sighed and followed Chris out Chantal's front door. "I hope you're right."

⸺✶⸺

Jon's body trembled as he climbed the narrow set of stairs leading to Mr. and Mrs. Davids' suite. He couldn't get arrested, not tonight, not after all he'd just been through with Alyssa. He could barely hear the noise from the scrambling party over of his pounding heartbeat. Praying that the door ahead of him would be unlocked, he turned the brass doorknob with ease.

Hustling into the suite, Jon locked the door behind him. If the police were going to arrest him, they would have to pick four or five locks. Without turning on a single light, he made his way across the bedroom and into a large bathroom. After locking the bathroom door, he opened another door that led to a dressing room. Jason's house was a maze and nearly impossible to travel through in darkness. Jon felt the wall next to the door in search of the light switch. Because the dressing room was windowless, there was no risk of the police seeing the light from outside. Jon's hand met with the switch as the dressing room illuminated with halogen lighting. Locking the door behind him, he crept further into the shelf-lined room. No one would find him in there, not even Jason. On the other hand, Jason was probably sitting in a police cruiser, claiming none of this was his fault.

As Jon sat down in a plush chair, a picture of Alyssa flashed into his mind. It was amazing how abruptly their relationship had ended. Jon had no regrets, however, except for possibly embarrassing himself. Nevertheless, he was confident that their breakup would not be the biggest gossip around school, since half of MLH's students were probably getting arrested.

The cops had shown up at Jason's last party, but Jon, Jason, Chris, Bryan, Cathy, and Alyssa had hidden in the dressing room and escaped detection. If Alyssa did get arrested, Jon knew she would get slammed with community service. After sighting all the drugs and alcohol at the party, the police were sure to run drug tests on everyone they booked. Jon couldn't help but conclude that Alyssa deserved everything she had coming to her.

Jon hoped that Jason would get arrested—just to scare him a little. Partying had begun to govern his life. Jason was one of the most intelligent people Jon knew. Despite his recent obsession with weed and his painfully teasing nature, Jason was actually a really good friend. Jon hated seeing someone as gifted as Jason waste his time chasing after the empty promises of the world. He had so much talent and zero desire to do anything productive with it. However, Jon knew he had no right to judge Jason; he had also been walking a dark path for the past two years.

I will lead the blind by ways they have not known, along unfamiliar paths I will guide them; I will turn the darkness into light before them and make the rough places smooth. Jon sighed as he recalled the quote from the Bible that Chantal had emailed him the day before their breakup. Looking back, Jon wished his heart had been fertile enough to absorb the seeds Chantal had tried to plant. By then, his heart had already grown hard. The seeds had been quickly plucked away by the immorality he had welcomed into his life.

"Guy, I can hear the police sirens already," Marc said as he reduced the speed of his red Dodge truck to forty-five. "Do you want me to turn down his street? It's coming up."

"Yeah, dude, whatever," Chris answered from beside Marielle. He had conveniently offered Chantal shotgun. "I just can't get arrested tonight."

"Well, if we just drive down his street, they can't arrest us," Chantal reasoned.

"Chris has gotten in trouble for stupider stuff," Marc stated while glancing at Chris in the rearview mirror.

"Oh, my gosh!" Chantal exclaimed, sighting the commotion surrounding Jason's house. Sirens wailed from the numerous cop cars lining his street. Cars with people scrambling into them were peeling left and right out of his driveway. "My sister is going to get in so much trouble!"

"I didn't know there would be this many people here," Marielle said quietly, leaning forward and peering out the window.

"I don't know about this, Little D," Marc said, steering his truck into a neighboring driveway. "You're out of your mind if you get out of this truck. The cops will think you were at the party, and they'll take you in. They know you."

"And then they'll give me a drug test, and I'll be screwed," Chris finished, leaning back against his seat. "Why am I so pathetic?"

"Chris," Marielle comforted him, placing her hand on his shoulder, "no cop will arrest the mayor's daughter. Court's fine."

"Let's just get out of here," Chris spoke downheartedly while looking at his trembling hands.

"Good decision," Marc said and began backing the truck out of the driveway.

"So, what's our plan?" Chantal asked and turned around to face Marielle and Chris. "Are we going back to your house, Chris?"

Chris remained silent as he glanced out the small window to his left.

"I don't think we should," Marielle reasoned, sending a worried glance in Chris's direction.

"What? Were you just talking to me?" Chris asked.

Chantal nodded and flashed him a sympathetic smile.

"Just let me know where I'm dropping you off," Marc said.

"Oh, are you girls coming back to my place?" Chris asked.

"We could watch that movie," Marielle replied.

Chris's lips arched into a smile. "Well, then, uh, my place it is."

CHAPTER 16

Courtney leaned into Bryan and excitedly whispered, "I can't believe we're getting away with this."

"It's getting pretty quiet now," Bryan observed, thrusting a wool peacoat from his leg. "What time is it?"

"I don't know," Courtney answered carelessly, inching closer to Bryan's warm body.

"Where do you think Jon is?"

Courtney shrugged. "He won't get in much trouble if he gets arrested. He's completely sober."

"True," Bryan agreed, "but his mom would kill him."

"Well, whose parents wouldn't? My dad would be so embarrassed!"

"Ha! The mayor's daughter at a drug-infested bender," Bryan teased, playing with Courtney's soft hair. "You little rebel."

Courtney turned her head towards Bryan. "Hey," she whispered softly while reaching for Bryan's hand.

"Hey," Bryan reciprocated, taking her hand into his own. Wrapping his other arm around her shoulder, he gazed into her eyes. "I want to kiss you so badly," he admitted, squeezing her hand tightly.

"I'd like that, but—"

"—Shhh," Bryan hushed, lightly brushing his lips against hers.

Courtney pulled away from him. "What about Chris?"

"If you want me to stop, I will," Bryan offered. "It will be really hard for me to not try to kiss you again, but it's up to you."

"I don't want to cheat on Chris," Courtney replied. "It wouldn't be fair."

"Whatever you want, Court," Bryan surrendered willingly and patted the top of her head.

While Courtney and Bryan were escaping detection at Jason's, Chris was climbing out of Marc's truck in front of his house. "Thanks, bro," he said. "Hey, are you sure you don't want to keep Chantal company?"

Marc smirked. "Dude, she's fifteen years old!"

"I hate to break it to you, but you're only seventeen, Marky-Marc," Chris laughed, raising his eyebrows in Chantal's direction. "She's hot."

"No, dude. Thanks, but I have plans tonight," Marc replied while glancing at the front steps where Chantal and Marielle were waiting. "I'm going to catch up with Michelle

Taylor and them. They avoided Matt and Luke's party, too—smart girls."

"Okay, whatever," Chris said and shrugged.

"Unless you want to come out with us?" Marc offered. "My friends thought you were cool at the concert."

"I was stoned at the concert," Chris stated, sounding ashamed. "I'm all through with that crap."

"Seriously?" Marc asked, raising his eyebrows in surprise.

Chris nodded. "I might be getting pulled up to JV, and I don't want to mess that up. No more weed, shrooms, tabs, alcohol, or anything. I'm all set."

Marc eyed Chris skeptically. "I've been waiting too long to hear you say that."

"Yeah, I know," Chris said downheartedly. "I don't want to follow Taylor's footsteps."

At the sound of his oldest brother's name, Marc's facial expression fell. "No. None of us do."

"Honestly, I don't even know if I would be standing here right now if you hadn't helped me out a few months ago," Chris admitted. "I don't even want to think about the stuff I used to do."

Marc sighed. "You were exposed to things at way too young of an age. Taylor never should have thrown all those parties while you were home. Don't beat yourself up over the past; just do your best to straighten out."

"I've come a long way, but I have a long way to go," Chris said. He knew that wanting to get sober and actually staying sober were two very different things. "I want to score it big with Marielle, and she doesn't need a drug-bag boyfriend. I'm trying to quit smoking, too. I don't think it suits me very well."

Marc laughed. "I don't think it suits anyone well. Pass Chantal my number and tell her to shoot me a text," he said while revving his engine.

"Will do," Chris replied before shutting the passenger-side door.

<hr>

"He is hitting on you *so* bad," Chantal whispered to Marielle as they waited for Chris on his front steps.

"Na-uh," Marielle denied, although she knew Chantal was right.

"Oh, p-lease," Chantal giggled.

"He's Courtney's boyfriend!" Marielle exclaimed loudly.

"Not for long," Chris whispered in Marielle's ear as he snuck up behind her.

Marielle shrieked, jumping and reddening with embarrassment.

"I'm sorry. Did I scare you?" Chris laughed and reached past Marielle to unlock his front door.

"You have no idea," Marielle responded, catching her breath as she followed Chris inside.

"Wow! Your house looks a lot cleaner than I expected," Chantal stated as she entered his home. "Aren't your parents away?"

"Yup," Chris replied carelessly while leading the girls into his immaculate, country kitchen. "Want something to eat?" he offered while opening his cabinets for any trace of food.

"Looks like the party really cleaned you out, huh?" Chantal commented as she opened the refrigerator.

"Ye-ah," Chris concluded gradually. "We can order takeout if you want?"

"I'm all set," Chantal said as her eyes met with the clock. "Seeing that it's eleven, we should probably start the movie."

Marielle nodded in agreement. "Chantal, how are we getting back to your house?"

A look of concern crept over Chantal's face. "Marc?" she asked.

"No," Chris shook his head, "he just left to chill with his crew."

"Uh, that's not good," Chantal responded.

"You guys could stay over!" Chris exclaimed, widening his bright, blue eyes.

"I don't think so," Marielle replied, staring at him in disbelief.

"No, really!" Chris cried. "Chantal, you've slept over my house before. If your mom let you then, she'll let you now."

"Chris," Chantal said, shaking her head, "we were twelve, and your parents were home. Besides, I slept in Katie's room with, like, five other girls."

"So, *you* can sleep in Katie's room if it will make you feel better," Chris laughed.

"You're a jerk," Chantal stated flatly and glanced from Chris to Marielle.

Marielle sighed. "If I end up sleeping over, you can consider me grounded for life. I am going to be in trouble when my mom finds out I was in a car tonight, anyway."

"How's she going to find out about that?" Chris asked, walking up behind her.

"She finds out about everything," Marielle replied, rolling her eyes. "It's her 'mother's intuition.' Besides, I just got done being grounded."

"Will you be grounded when your 'mother's intuition' finds out that I kissed you?" Chris asked and turned her around to face him.

"Huh?" Marielle questioned him, widening her eyes in confusion.

Chris lifted Marielle's chin and smiled slightly. Closing his eyes, he pressed his lips softly against hers. Marielle pushed Chris away and widened her eyes in awe. Slowly, a smile began spreading across her lips. Although there were hundreds of questions racing through her mind, she remained silent.

"Chris, can I go use your bathroom?" Chantal asked timidly, darting her eyes from Marielle to Chris.

"The one upstairs is cleaner," Chris replied and winked at Chantal.

"Oh, of course it is." Chantal rolled her eyes and nudged Marielle as she exited the kitchen.

"What was that for?" Marielle asked, warily eyeing Chris.

"Why'd you stop me?" Chris asked, taking a step in her direction.

"You're Courtney's boyfriend!" Marielle exclaimed, reminding herself of how wrong the situation was.

"I'd rather be yours," Chris admitted with a shrug.

Marielle sighed, slumped onto a chair, and rested her arms on the kitchen table.

Yesterday, the first day of school, she had spotted Chris in her biology class. He had sat towards the back of the lab with Jason, Cathy, and Leslie. Marielle had only begun watching him because she wanted to look out for Courtney. She had the preconceived notion that Chris was a player, and she had expected him to do something to disrespect their relationship. To her surprise, Chris had seemed oblivious to Cathy and Leslie's existence. He took notes during class and appeared genuinely interested in what their teacher was saying. From the way Courtney had described him, Marielle had never expected him to care about school. She found herself perplexed by his good behavior. He did not seem anything like the "bad-boy" Courtney had described to her.

Marielle had grown surprisingly jealous of Courtney as she continued to observe Chris. He had glanced up from his notebook towards the end of class and caught Marielle staring at him. She had immediately turned bright red and dropped her eyes to the floor. He was smiling at her when she looked back up, and she finally realized why girls made such a big deal out of him: he had one of the most beautiful smiles she had ever seen.

Escaping from her daze, Marielle realized she was sitting in Chris's kitchen with him eyeing her expectantly. She could not believe he had more interest in her than Courtney. Every guy wanted Courtney.

It was sweet how concerned Chris had been about Courtney, but what had transformed him into a cheater? Had Marielle been right all along? Was Chris truly the player she had first judged him to be? Did she dare get involved with someone so fickle?

She immediately felt bad for even entertaining the idea. The charming, blue-eyed boy staring at her was her best friend's boyfriend. That was a line Marielle never wanted to cross, even in her thoughts.

CHAPTER 17

Bryan nudged Courtney in her side. "Court," he whispered. "Court, wake up."

"What?" Courtney yawned, squinting her eyes open. "What time is it?"

"I don't know. I fell asleep," Bryan said while staring admiringly at her.

"Oh, my gosh! I was supposed to sleep at Alyssa's!" Courtney recalled, sitting up straight. "Is it morning or still night?"

"It's probably safe to go check," Bryan reasoned. "I doubt there are any cops around. Shifts change, and this place cleared out fast."

"I'm still half-asleep," Courtney said, thrusting jackets off her lap. "Where are we again?"

"Under Jason's stairs."

"Right," she groaned, recalling the events of the party.

"Did you ever call Chris back?"

"He was supposed to call us. I hope he didn't come all the way out here because he couldn't get through to me."

"Would he do that?"

"I don't know."

"I'd do that for you."

Courtney smiled. "I believe that. Now, lead me out of this closet."

"Come on," Bryan said, grasping Courtney's hand.

Seconds later, they cautiously emerged from the closet. Moonlight lit the foyer as it shone through the large palladium window. The room appeared empty and the mansion deserted. Still hesitant, Courtney and Bryan crept through the room, warily eyeing their surroundings. Bryan tugged on Courtney's left hand and pointed to the kitchen's French doors. Tiptoeing into the room, they found it deserted and piled high with party debris.

"Boy did I pick a bad year to quit smoking," Bryan stated with a short laugh as he picked a large bag of marijuana up off the floor. "I wonder why the cops didn't take this?"

"There was so much that maybe they missed it?" Courtney suggested.

"No, it probably wasn't here when they searched the place," Bryan reasoned. "I bet people hid all throughout this house."

"Well, if, uh, that clock's right, then it's 2:30 a.m.," Courtney said, pointing to Jason's microwave.

"How did you leave things with your parents?" Bryan asked and leaned against the granite counter. "Were you supposed to check in at a certain time?"

"Uh, no. They were supposed to call me if they needed me."

"That's funny, 'cause your phone was shut off half the night," Bryan stated without laughing.

Courtney's eyes widened. "I hope they didn't call Alyssa's parents! That would be really bad because my parents didn't know I was leaving her house."

"Do they have her number?" Bryan asked.

"Come on, my dad's the mayor!" Courtney exclaimed. "Not to mention my sister has been dating Alyssa's brother for five years! I think they'll make the Alyssa Kelly/John Kelly connection."

"Well, Alyssa's in jail, so ten-to-one her parents are at the police station."

"Ten-to-one my dad's at the police station," Courtney stated, pondering her options. "I should call Chris and try to get us a ride out of here."

"Call him, and I'll call Jon," Bryan said. "I know he's either still here or at home 'cause that big bag of weed was his."

"And you know this how?" Courtney questioned him suspiciously.

"Don't look at me like that, Court. I told you I don't smoke anymore," Bryan stressed. "I only know it's Jon's because I saw him bag it with Jason after school. Jay sealed it with a ribbon. Who else ties a quarter with a ribbon?"

Courtney shrugged. "You got me there. Well, at least we know Jon didn't get arrested. Why did he break up with Alyssa if he does that crap, too?"

"Jon doesn't do drugs," Bryan stated flatly.

"He wasn't going to deal it, was he?" Courtney asked.

Bryan shook his head. "No. Chris gave Jason the money for it on Wednesday night, so Jason gave it to Jon to give to Chris. Jay and Chris aren't on speaking terms at the moment, so Jon was going to deliver it to him. Sorry to tell you, but your boyfriend has a little bit of a drug problem."

"I don't get why he bothers with drugs," Courtney said. "It's not cool, it's not attractive, and it ruins relationships. When I started going out with him, I had no idea he was a stoner. And people wonder why I don't still like him? Maybe he's trying to change, or maybe he's just distant because of his fight with Jay? I honestly don't know. I just want our relationship back, Bry."

Bryan blushed and wrapped his arms around Courtney. "Well, this time I don't want to lose you."

"This time you won't," Courtney whispered into his ear.

Around the same time, Cathy was inside her own home, angrily questioning her parents. "Okay, so what, am I grounded?"

"Boy, is that an understatement!" her father laughed.

"Cathaleen, what made you do this?" her mother asked, while staring at her in awe.

"Do what, Mom?" Cathy responded in annoyance. "Do I suddenly not measure up to Chantal? Am I not the perfect little angel I've led you to believe I am?"

"Cathy, we just want to know what has influenced you," her father pressed. "Whether you see it as wrong or not, getting arrested is not going to please us. Not to mention that you lied and said you were sleeping at Alyssa's."

"I would have slept at Alyssa's after the party if the cops hadn't shown up," Cathy replied without remorse. "So, don't even say I lied!"

"You never mentioned a party to us," her mother stated.

"Oh, so it would have been okay if I had 'mentioned' the party?" Cathy mocked her. "You know how out of control Jason's brothers can get. You wouldn't have let me go to the party if I had asked you for permission. Jason's my boyfriend. I had to be there."

Mrs. Kagelli sighed. "You can deal with her, Michael. I'm going to bed. I never thought she and Chantal could grow so far apart," she said and left the room in dismay.

CHAPTER 18

<u>Marielle Kayne—2:30 a.m.</u>

I have told Courtney a countless number of times that she was crazy to break up with Bryan Sartelli for Chris Dunkin. I was only giving my opinion—you know, trying to be a good best friend. But now, after Courtney finds out that I slept over Chris's house, she is not going to think I was being a good friend. In fact, she'll probably think I was after her boyfriend the entire time. I mean, why wouldn't she?

<u>Bryan Sartelli—2:30 a.m.</u>

I'm glad Courtney believed me when I told her that I still love her. She says she's going to break up with Chris for me, but that could just be a line of bull.

I don't think she has a clue what she wants. She's been acting kind of crazy lately. I'm shocked she showed up with Alyssa tonight. The Courtney I dated did not become friends with girls like Alyssa. I'm guessing Courtney felt uncomfortable at the party, so it's good I took her upstairs to talk. I bet she understands now what I meant when I told her my friends are no good. She always fought me on that. That's cool she didn't cheat on Chris because I can assume she never cheated on me. Seriously though, Courtney needs to get her priorities straight. I said I'd never let her hurt me again, but I'm a stupid kid.

⸺✷⸺

"Dude, it's like three in the morning. What the heck are you doing here?!" Chris exclaimed as he opened his front door and let Marc inside his home.

"I didn't feel like driving all the way home," Marc replied while walking into the living room. "Oh, hey. You girls are still here?"

"Yeah, we're staying over," Chantal said and smiled brightly.

Marc smirked. "Oh, sorry to interrupt," he joked and nudged Chris.

Chris rolled his eyes and shook his head, hoping Marc's comment had not embarrassed the girls. Evidently Chantal's parents had an "emergency" arise at home, which caused them to agree to the sleepover. Chris assumed their emergency had something to do with Cathy's attendance at Jason's party.

"How's your girlfriend, Little D?" Marc questioned him and sat down beside Chantal on the love seat.

"You're killin' me, Smalls," Chris replied, shaking his head and walking over to the sofa where Marielle was sitting. He hesitated slightly before putting his muscular arm around her shoulders. Marielle, who seemed half-asleep, leaned into Chris's chest.

"Where's Katie?" Marc asked, taking off his leather sandals.

"Upstairs sleeping," Chris replied. "Unless you woke her up when you peeled onto my street."

"Oh, sorry," Marc apologized, leaning back against the love seat, slightly in Chantal's direction. "I didn't even realize it was so late."

"Where'd you go after you dropped us off?" Chantal asked.

"I just met up with some friends. It was pretty lowkey. I was the DD, so I couldn't drink. What have you guys been up to?"

"We just watched a movie," Chantal replied.

"So, what's going on with them?" Marc whispered, leaning in closer to Chantal. "Are they together now or something?"

"I'm sure they would be if I wasn't here making the situation awkward."

"Maybe we should leave them alone?"

"And go where?"

Marc shrugged. "Wherever you want."

"Well, do you mean, like, in another room or, like, out somewhere?"

"It's kind of late, but if you want to go for a drive, we can," Marc offered.

The telephone began ringing loudly, causing everyone to jump in their seats.

"Who is seriously calling my house this late?" Chris asked, while reaching past Marielle for the cordless phone. "Hello?"

"Hi, um, is Chris there?" a hesitant voice responded.

"That's me," Chris replied.

"Oh, hi," the girl said awkwardly. "It's Courtney."

Chris's heart sank. Courtney was one of the last people he wanted to talk to while sitting beside Marielle. "Oh, hi, Court," he greeted her, watching Marielle's facial expression grow tense. "Where are you?"

"Bryan and I are at Jason's. The cops came, but we hid from them in a closet. I was pretty scared, but Bryan knew what to do."

I'm sure he did. "You know, I came looking for you around eleven. The cops were there, so I didn't go inside. Let me ask, why are you just calling me now?"

"Bryan and I sort of fell asleep, but nothing happened, Chris—I swear! Really, you know I would never cheat on you."

"Right," Chris said quietly, wishing something had happened so he would have an excuse to break up with her.

"Are you okay? I didn't wake you up, did I?"

"No, you didn't wake any of us up. Marc, Chantal, Marielle, and I are all wide awake."

"Marielle and Chantal are still with you?" Courtney questioned him with a pang of jealousy present in her tone. "What are you guys doing?"

"Just chillin'. They're spending the night."

"Oh," Courtney commented awkwardly.

"Does that bother you?" Chris asked, detecting the uneasiness of her tone.

"No," Courtney said. "It's just random, I guess. I mean, do you even know Marielle?"

Courtney was clueless, and that only made the conversation more uncomfortable for Chris. Was he positive he wanted to break up with her? If he was, should he do it in person or right then on the phone? He had plenty of reasons to break up with her. In fact, she was probably expecting a breakup.

"Court, we need to talk," was all he could think to say.

"I know," Courtney agreed, "but can you guys come get us first? I'm really scared the cops are going to come back with my dad or something. Would your cousin mind coming out this late?"

CHAPTER 19

ryan let out a sigh of relief as he watched Jon enter the kitchen. "I knew you were still here," he said while walking away from Courtney, who was still on the phone with Chris.

"Who's she on the phone with?" Jon asked, gesturing towards Courtney as he hopped up onto the counter.

"Chris," Bryan replied. "Marc may still be able to pick us up."

"Really?" Jon inquired. "Do you think he'll get me, too? I was wondering how I was going to get home. Where do you think Jay is?"

Bryan shrugged. "I have no idea what happened to Jay or anyone else. He probably took off with Luke or Matt. The Davids are pros at getting out of trouble. I'm sure Marc will let us ride in the body of his truck. I just don't know how happy Chris is with Courtney or me."

"Oooh, what happened?" Jon sang curiously.

Bryan shrugged.

"Did you score?" Jon whispered, raising his eyebrows in Courtney's direction.

"Courtney's not like that," Bryan replied quickly. "Even when we were together."

"Ah, don't worry about it, guy. I'm not going to be getting any play now either," Jon said. "I can't believe I broke up with Alyssa tonight. Next week was going to be our thirteen-month anniversary. I really hope I don't regret it."

"Don't worry about that," Bryan stressed. "Alyssa's gone way downhill since you two got together. You know she's not the same girl we used to chill with. She's one of the last people I want Courtney becoming friends with. Besides, you said last week that you were only staying with her because she's good in bed. I know you want more than that. We know plenty of girls who would jump in your pants without a second thought. If you were just looking for sex, you'd stay single and play around."

"You're right," Jon agreed. "I did pretty well before Alyssa. We didn't even have sex, and I was happy. I was an idiot to let her go."

Bryan nodded in agreement, knowing that Jon was referring to Chantal. He always referred to Chantal. Jon might have caused their relationship to end, but Bryan knew Jon had never let her go.

"They're coming," Courtney sang, interrupting Bryan's thoughts. "Chris said only Marc is coming, so we can all fit in his truck."

<u>Julianna Camen—3:00 a.m.</u>

It's not just me being insecure when I say that the whole world has forgotten about me. Courtney is out with her new friends, Marielle is sleeping over Chantal Kagelli's, and I am at home with nothing to do. Perhaps I am just feeling sorry for myself, or perhaps I've come to the conclusion that I have no true friends at all.

After Marc and Chantal left for Jason's house, Marielle lay with Chris on the couch. Being so close to him brought about a queasy feeling in her stomach. After a bit of resistance, Marc had been able to convince Chantal to accompany him to Jason's. Marielle assumed that Marc had interest in Chantal but was unable to decipher if it was mutual. Marc was gorgeous, but Chantal was clearly the loyal type, leaving Andy Rosetti without any concern.

Chantal seemed to have better morals than anyone in Marielle's life. After allowing Chris to hit on her so blatantly, Marielle wondered if she appeared malicious to Chantal. After all, Marielle was Courtney's best friend. Alyssa had been Chantal's best friend until she fell for Jon behind Chantal's back. Jon had been Chantal's boyfriend until he cheated on her with Alyssa. Marielle swallowed deeply, realizing she was treading in very dangerous water.

"How do you think this is going to go down?" Chris asked, resting the back of his head in his hands and glancing up at the ceiling.

"What?"

"Well, you know, us and Courtney," Chris clarified while turning to face Marielle.

"I don't know," Marielle replied, holding her gaze steadily on the ceiling.

"I mean, what are we really?" Chris rambled, setting his eyes on her. "I've made it obvious that I like you, but I have no idea how you feel about me."

Marielle rolled onto her side to face Chris. "I like you in the same way," she admitted, "and I would like to hang out again, but that really isn't an option. You have a girlfriend—my best friend—who is on her way to your house right now. It's not even right for us to talk about liking each other."

Chris nodded and tore his blue eyes off Marielle. "How about we just play it by ear and see how things go when she gets here?"

"Fine," Marielle agreed, doubting a positive outcome.

⬥

<u>Julianna Camen—3:15 a.m.</u>
I wonder what everyone would think if I ran away?

⬥

"Hey, Chantal. I didn't expect to see you," Jon greeted her as he climbed into the backseat of Marc's truck.

"Oh," Chantal replied, sounding more tired than friendly as she avoided eye contact with him.

120

"Jon, you can put my gym bag on the floor if it will give you guys more room," Marc said.

"Hi, Chantal. Hi, Marc," Bryan called out, following Jon into the truck. "Thanks for picking us up so late."

"We came by earlier, but the 5-Os were everywhere," Marc explained.

"That's what Chris said," Courtney stated as she sat down beside Bryan.

"You must be Courtney," Marc said. "I'm Marc, Chris's cousin, and this is Chantal, but you probably know her already."

"No, I don't," Courtney responded in a friendly tone. "Well, it's nice to meet you guys. Thanks for coming both times."

"No problem," Marc said and turned to face Chantal. "We wanted to take a drive anyway."

"Are we all going back to Chris's?" Courtney asked as Marc backed his truck out of Jason's driveway.

"My house is on the way if you want to drop me off," Jon said.

"You live one street over from Chris, right?" Marc recalled.

"Yeah," Jon responded.

"I can drop you off," Marc agreed. "Anyone else?"

"You can bring me home if you want," Courtney said.

"No, not you, Courtney. You and Chris need to talk," Marc stated with a short laugh.

As they approached Jon's neighborhood about ten minutes later, Jon pointed to a spot where he wanted to be dropped off. "You can just stop at the end of my street. Yeah, right here," he directed Marc. "Thanks, dude. I'll give Chris some gas money for ya."

"Don't worry about it," Marc responded and leaned his seat forward so Jon could exit the truck.

"Bye, guys," Jon said, pausing for a second to look at Chantal.

"Later," Marc and Bryan called in unison as Jon shut the driver-side door.

Jon watched the truck drive down the main road until it disappeared onto Chris's street. Seeing Chantal always messed with his head. A huge part of him wanted to run to Chris's and find out how she had ended up with Marc. More than anything he wanted an opportunity to discuss their mess of a breakup. He sighed, knowing he did not deserve a moment of her attention.

Turning right onto his street, Jon heard a faint sound in the distance. Footsteps maybe? Or a stray dog? Whatever it was continued to move slowly in his direction.

"Hello?" Jon called out into the warm September air. The footsteps halted abruptly. "Who's that?" he asked while moving towards the figure he was unable to recognize. Surely, it's a person, he thought. Maybe someone from Jason's party?

"Who are you?" a timid female voice asked.

Jon continued to move towards the stranger and then halted at a ten-foot distance. Slowly, the girl moved closer to Jon until their distance had diminished to a few feet.

Jon studied the stranger in the faint starlight. "Julianna?" he asked, recognizing the girl from school.

"Hi," Julianna said quietly. "You're one of Courtney's new friends, huh?"

"I'm Jon," he introduced himself and stepped closer to her. "We're in the same computer class. You were the only girl I didn't know. What are you doing out here at 3:30 in the morning?"

Julianna shrugged. "It's a really long story. Please excuse me," she said and pushed past him.

"Where are you going?" Jon called out after her.

Julianna turned around and stared curiously at Jon. "What's it to you?"

"Well, maybe I'd like to come," Jon responded and walked over to her.

"No, you wouldn't," Julianna stated assuredly. "I'm going nowhere in particular."

"Me either," Jon said. "I was supposed to spend the night at my friend's house. I just got dropped off from his party because it got crashed. Do you know Jay Davids?"

Julianna nodded. "He's one of Courtney's new friends."

"Do you keep referring to Courtney Angeletti?"

"Yeah. She was my best friend for ten years."

Jon lowered his eyebrows in confusion. He never would have correlated Courtney with the timid girl before his eyes. "No way, seriously? What happened with that?" Jon asked and sat down on the concrete curb.

"I went away this summer with my family. When I came back, she wasn't my friend anymore," Julianna replied and sat down beside Jon. "She broke up with Bryan, the sweetest kid she'd ever gone out with, and started going out with his friend Chris. That was the end of our friendship."

"Wow, real nice," Jon stated sarcastically, realizing how ironic and random their conversation was.

"I guess Courtney thinks she's too popular for me or Marielle now that she's friends with Alyssa Kelly and Cathy Kagelli."

Jon laughed. "Well, here's a news flash for you: Courtney is about to break up with Chris for Bryan; I just broke up with Alyssa; Cathy and Alyssa both got arrested tonight; and Marielle is sleeping over Chris's… Shall I go on?"

"What?!" Julianna exclaimed as if Jon had been speaking gibberish. "Marielle doesn't even know Chris Dunkin."

"I bet she does now."

"You're making no sense. How did Courtney end up with Bryan?"

"Now that's a long story," Jon said while standing up from the curb. "Let's go for a walk," he suggested and helped Julianna to her feet.

⊷⊶

"Chantal, can you wait here for a minute?" Marc asked after Courtney and Bryan climbed out of his truck.

Chantal turned towards Marc. "What's up?"

"Well, I was just wondering if we're going to talk again after tonight?" Marc asked.

"I'd like that," Chantal replied, "but Chris told you that I have a boyfriend, right?"

Marc shook his head. "No, but that's okay. We didn't do anything wrong."

"It doesn't bother you?"

"Well, sure, it makes me a little sad, but as long as we can be friends, I'm cool with it," Marc replied. "Your boyfriend's lucky. Who is he?"

"Andy Rosetti," Chantal replied. "You might know his older brother, Robby. He's a senior, too."

"Oh, yeah, I do," Marc nodded in recognition. "Actually, I know Andy, too. He's a good kid. Robby came to that concert with Chris and me a few weeks ago. I was actually out with him earlier tonight."

Chantal smiled. "We'll keep in touch, Marc… and I think we have a very interesting night ahead of us."

CHAPTER 20

<u>Chantal Kagelli—4:00 a.m.</u>

His ways are not our ways, and His thoughts are not our thoughts. I have no idea how I ended up having such a whirlwind of a night, but I feel like a lot of things are being brought to light. I'm not even going to try to make sense of it. I'm certain that God has His hand in this entire fiasco.

<u>Marielle Kayne—4:00 a.m.</u>

Everything happens for a reason. If Chantal hadn't invited me to sleep over, then I would never be spending the night at Chris's. If Courtney hadn't gone to the party, I would never be spending the night at Chris's. If Chris had gone to the party, I would never be spending the night at his house, and if Courtney wasn't my best friend, I wouldn't feel so guilty.

⸺⊰✦⊱⸺

Jon eyed Julianna sympathetically as they strolled along through the still September night. "So, how long are you planning to run away?"

"Just for a day or so… to get some attention."

"Well, you're already getting my attention," Jon stated.

Julianna blushed. "Thanks."

"You know," Jon began, "I don't think running away from Montgomery is going to solve any of your problems. I think what you need to do is face Courtney, face your parents, and face anything else that's bothering you. Stop with all the insecure nonsense and stand up for yourself."

"O-kay," Julianna said hesitantly.

"No, Julianna. Seriously, I mean what I say," Jon pressed. "You can't see it, but I can see how great your life could be. Just listen to what I'm saying. Courtney is obviously being self-centered. She is wrong, not you, so why should you be the one suffering?"

"Courtney has a gift called popularity," Julianna retorted. "If you're friends with her, you obviously know. You have the same gift."

"So, what? Her popularity intimidates you?"

"How can I put it? Courtney's prideful attitude makes me nauseous," Julianna spat.

"Okay, that works," Jon laughed, surprised by her bold response.

"You're right though. I should confront her," Julianna admitted. "Her and everyone else. I'm the only one who can make myself happy."

"No, now that's where you are wrong," Jon challenged her in a playful tone.

"What do you mean?" Julianna asked, sounding off-put.

"Well, I think I could make you happy."

Julianna stopped walking for a second and then continued side-by-side with Jon.

Jon laughed. "Now you're being the snob!" he exclaimed. "What, you have no response to my offer?"

"Offer? I thought you were challenging me."

Jon shrugged without pausing next to her. "That, too," he admitted.

"So, what are you saying?" Julianna asked as she caught up to him.

"What do you think about making an appearance at Chris's love-triangle sleepover?" Jon offered. "Courtney's there, and I can guarantee she won't be feeling very 'popular.' Chris stayed home with Marielle instead of going to pick up Courtney. That tells me Courtney is about to get dumped."

"But I thought she wants to break up with Chris for Bryan?"

"True, but she's totally sweating the idea," Jon said. "I mean, after all, she's pretty crazy."

Julianna laughed.

"So, you agree with me now?!" Jon exclaimed triumphantly.

"On that note," Julianna nodded, still laughing.

"Oh, you are coming with me to Chris's, Julianna Camen!" Jon sang and spread an amused smirk across his lips.

"Okay," Julianna agreed willingly. "But why are you helping me? You're Courtney's friend. Shouldn't you be defending her?"

Jon shook his head. "When I broke up with Alyssa tonight, Courtney sided with her. All of our other friends knew better than to say a word. Then we got separated for, like, three hours after the cops showed up. Are you following me?"

Julianna nodded.

"After the cops left, I met up with Bryan and Court in the kitchen. She was on the phone with Chris, figuring out how she could get home. When she hung up with Chris, she started yelling at me for embarrassing Alyssa. So right now, she's not my favorite person," Jon explained while leading Julianna onto Chris's street. "So, running into you was priceless."

"That's so typical of Courtney. She can't keep her opinion to herself."

"I thought she was a pretty cool chic, before tonight anyway, so I told Alyssa to become friends with her," Jon said. "All the guys are getting pretty sick of Alyssa and Cathy. I figured because they all like Courtney, they'd like Alyssa more if she hung out with her. That didn't work, so now you're my new favorite girl."

"What?!" Julianna exclaimed and glared at Jon.

"Well, it's a tossup between you and Chantal," Jon added, ignoring the cold stare she'd set upon him.

"Oh, that is enough!" Julianna scoffed. "Do you think I'm too upset to see what you're trying to do? Do you think I'm going to ignore what I've heard you're about?" With that Julianna sprinted into the darkness of Chris's street.

Jon groaned and began running after her. "I didn't mean it like that," he yelled into the night's air.

CHAPTER 21

Inside Chris's home, Marc, Chantal, Bryan, and Marielle settled in to watch a movie, while Chris led Courtney upstairs.

"Courtney, this isn't working," Chris stated as he shut his bedroom door behind them.

Courtney nodded in agreement and sat down at the foot of Chris's king-size bed.

"It's not your fault, and I don't think it's mine either. It's just, as boyfriend and girlfriend, we don't mesh very well," Chris reasoned, sitting down beside her.

Courtney remained silent, failing to tear her eyes off the floor.

"Court, the last thing I want to do is hurt you," Chris said, placing a comforting hand on her shoulder. "I mean you're an inspiration to me, and you're one of my best friends. You saved me, Court. You got me to care about my life again. No one else has ever made such an impact on me. I don't know where I would be if I hadn't met you. God blessed me the day you came into my life."

Courtney glanced up at Chris with tears in her eyes. "Thanks," she mumbled.

"No, thank you," Chris stressed. "I care about you a lot, Court, and I want you to always be a part of my life."

"Yeah?"

"And I know how you feel about Bryan, but I accept that," he added.

"You… you do?" Courtney stammered, sounding more surprised than relieved.

"Yeah. We rushed into things. I should have given you more time to get over him, you know, before I swept you off your feet," Chris joked and winked at her. "It was just that, when I met you, I knew there was something special about you, and I had to find out what. It turns out I was right about something for once in my messed-up life. People probably thought I asked you out because you're beautiful and fun, but no offense, that wasn't what I was looking for."

Courtney looked surprised. "What do you mean?"

"At Jon's beach party, you stayed dead sober around a bunch of drunk kids and still had a good time. That was the first night I met you, and I was floored by your strength. Being the loser I am, I asked if you wanted to get high. You were like, 'No. Drugs are against my religious beliefs. They don't interest me.' I remember thinking, *I want that strength*. At that time, I was drinking or getting high every single day. I felt like I needed to, and I hated my dependency. That's when I realized what I was looking for: I wanted an out from my own lifestyle. When I saw you, it hit me. You were my inspiration."

Courtney lowered her eyebrows and listened intently to Chris.

"I knew I couldn't do it alone because I am a very weak person. The more time I spent with you, the less dependent I felt on drugs. I was doing so much better until I agreed to have that party the other night. I fell right back into my old ways. I woke up still drunk, realizing I had blacked out at the party. That's when something clicked. If I really want to straighten out my life, I have to stay away from my friends. That's why I cancelled the party, and that's what I wanted to talk to you about at lunch today."

Courtney sat in silence, taking a moment to register the emotional bomb Chris had just dropped on her. Even though Chris's words were complimentary, words that could have enlarged Courtney's ego, she was saddened by his confession.

"Oh, Chris, I am so sorry," she said after a moment. "I should have heard you out. Instead of being the inspiration you needed, I fueled the fire. There you were trying to escape from your friends with me, and there I was ditching you for them. Wow. That's..." She put her hands to her tear-streaked face and took a deep breath. She shook her head from side to side, attempting to grasp the depth of her own shallow behavior. "That's... geez... that's awful," she finished.

Chris draped his arm around Courtney. "I wasn't trying to make you upset. I was just trying to explain myself to you. I'm sorry."

"No, please do not be sorry," she stressed, pulling away from Chris's embrace. "You just made me realize how lost I've become. I'm so touched by the impact you think I had on your life."

"Good, I want you to be. I want you to realize how much you've done for me."

"Don't you get it, though? You went after the wrong person," Courtney said matter-of-factly.

"What are you talking about?" Chris laughed. "I went after you. I went after you even though you were dating one of my best friends. Can't you see how selfish I am?"

Courtney laughed. "Like I said, you went after the wrong person. You saw strength in me and said, 'I want that!' so you went after me. But look at me now. Look at how quickly I let you down. Don't you get it? I am only human; what you saw in me was something much greater. The strength you want can't come from me," she explained. "That strength only comes from God."

Chris lowered his eyebrows and swallowed the lump in his throat that had grown with every word Courtney spoke. *What the heck is she talking about?*

"I'm usually the first to take credit for something, but even I know my limits. I haven't been to church lately, and I haven't been praying either. I got too wrapped up in my social life to think about spiritual things. What you just said made me realize how quickly I lost my strength by being away from God. Do you know I even smoked part of a cigarette today?" Courtney admitted.

Chris laughed. "That'd be a sight to see! That's not the Courtney I know."

"Yeah, well, Alyssa said you told her I smoked, so I felt like I had to."

"I never said anything like that. I would never make up a lie about you. She was probably just trying to test you," Chris said and rolled his eyes. "Alyssa doesn't even smoke."

Courtney shrugged. "It doesn't matter now anyway. I'm over it. But it just goes to show how weak I've become. Saying no to drugs and voicing my beliefs was never hard for me when God was at the center of my life. I've also grown a hardened heart toward people who were once my close friends," she admitted.

Chris let out a deep breath. "So, you're saying what I saw in you was the strength you got from God, and that is what drew me to you?"

Courtney nodded. "I think we both misunderstood why we were drawn to each other. It was supernatural."

"I believe in God. I'm Catholic," Chris stated flatly. "How can you go to a party and not even have one drink, and I can't even avoid alcohol in my own home?"

Courtney let out a heavy breath. "That's a loaded question," she said and paused for a second, appearing to gather her thoughts. "There's a difference between believing in God and having a relationship with Him. Last year, I saw a huge change in my sister for the better, and I became curious about the cause. She told me that when she started going to church with her boyfriend, it changed her life. I didn't get it; we had gone to church our whole lives, so what made the difference? She invited me to come and see for myself. That was when I accepted Christ."

"Like, you got communion?"

"No," Courtney said and shook her head. "I accepted God's forgiveness."

"Did you go to confession?"

"No, it wasn't anything formal."

"Then how did you 'accept Christ?' What does that even mean?"

Courtney eyed him thoughtfully before beginning to speak. "The gospel was explained in a way I could understand. I realized that God is able to forgive me for my sins because Jesus already paid the price for them when He died on the cross. That day, I turned my life over to God and asked the Holy Spirit to live inside me and use me for God's purpose. I'm pretty sure that's what you saw in me."

Chris stared at Courtney blankly.

"At my church, the pastors teach us how to connect with God and hear His voice," Courtney added.

Chris raised his eyebrows. "I didn't know that was even possible. I knew you were religious, but I didn't realize you were spiritual."

"I was before I got distracted."

"So, what you're saying is I'm already forgiven, and I don't need to go to confession?" Chris asked, squinting in confusion.

Courtney shook her head from side to side and let out a short laugh. "I'm sorry. This probably seems so random. I need to explain myself better." After clearing her throat, she said, "God used to require innocent blood to be shed for the atonement of sins. That's why the Jews did animal sacrifices in their temple. Then God promised them a new covenant: The Messiah. It was prophesied in Isaiah 53, and it happened.

Jesus willingly died on the cross to pay the penalty for our sins so we could spend eternity in Heaven. That is what I learned in church, and that is what the Bible says."

"I've never actually read the Bible," Chris admitted, realizing he knew very little about his own religion.

"Lately, I haven't done much more than live for myself," Courtney admitted with her chin quivering, "and I am so sorry I let you down."

Chris stared at Courtney in disbelief. He couldn't help but think, *What the heck just happened?* Yet, what she said made sense. Hearing her speak about her love for God brought Chris back to the first night he met her. He recalled being undeniably drawn to her, for a reason he couldn't explain. Of course she was beautiful, but he knew a lot of pretty girls who had never captivated him in that way. She hadn't been flirtatious either. *Could it really have been God drawing us together?*

Courtney was right; she had let Chris down. Once his inspiration became less inspiring, he had fallen right back to where he was before he met her. The thought had never crossed Chris's mind that his desires were of a spiritual nature. Up until this conversation, everything in his life seemed trivial. He really had no idea what the Bible said. It would be foolish to have an opinion about something he knew nothing about. What made Chris think there could be merit to Courtney's words was the strength he noticed in her from the very start—the strength he had watched fade as she drifted further and further from God and he became less and less attracted to her.

"Court, I'm sorry if dating me pulled you away from church," Chris apologized and hung his head.

"That's not your fault. I kept myself from going to church and reading the Bible. My pride, my vanity, and my ego got me really lost," Courtney stated assuredly.

"So, that makes sense. The reason why I felt less attracted to you was spiritual," Chris reasoned, taking Courtney's words to heart.

"Yeah, most likely," Courtney agreed, "but isn't that cool how attracted to God you were?"

Chris laughed. "Yeah. Someone must have been praying for me."

Courtney smiled.

"So, are you going to start going back to church?" Chris asked.

Courtney nodded. "Oh, yeah. I've seen the person I am without God, and I'm pretty ashamed."

Chris had never heard Courtney speak so humbly. The change he saw in her during that conversation alone was enough to make him want God in his life. All along he had gone after the wrong person.

"Would it be weird if I came with you sometime?" Chris asked. "Since we just broke up and all?"

"It would be awesome if you came with me to church," Courtney said and smiled warmly.

CHAPTER 22

Jon hustled toward Julianna. "Will you stop?!" he pleaded, finally catching up to the distressed girl.

"I'm sorry, Jon. I'm sorry," Julianna surrendered, slumping to the ground in front of Chris's house.

"You're a mess!" Jon exclaimed, while looking down at the sobbing girl. He barely knew her, but somehow, he felt involved in her life. She was unstable, stressed to the maximum, and getting on his last nerve. Nevertheless, Jon had already ruined one girl's night, and his conscience was not going to allow him to ruin another's. "Let me help you, please."

Julianna continued to sob and tightly grip her knees to her chest. Sighing, Jon did the only thing he could think to do: he knelt down and wrapped his arms around her. As he embraced her, his feelings of annoyance transformed into concern. What upset Julianna was greater than the petty problems he and his friends considered jeopardizing. Julianna's life was more complicated than most.

"You don't understand me," Julianna sobbed. "People actually want to be your friend."

She has a point, Jon concluded, but he knew he had to humble himself. "Julianna, you may think popularity comes easily to me, but I had no idea you felt that way until now. You see, you have no idea how people view you until you actually sit down and talk to them. You were the only girl who didn't say hi to me in class. Do you know what that made me think?"

Julianna shrugged.

"It made me wonder who you were. I made a mental note to sit near you next class so I could find out. I didn't think you were a loser just because you're not in my group of friends. I knew nothing about you, so how could I have an opinion of you? That would have been pretty stupid, and I don't like to think I'm stupid," Jon explained, taking Julianna's trembling hand. "You care too much about what other people think of you. If I cared about what people thought of me, I would probably have run away from Montgomery years ago."

Julianna lowered her eyebrows and pulled her hand out of Jon's grip. "Don't mock me!" she cried defensively.

Jon rolled his eyes. "I'm not mocking you; I'm being serious. Let me tell you a little secret about popularity. If you consider someone popular, they probably have no idea. People want to be around people who are real. Most likely those people don't even care about popularity. Now, I know there are some people who crave the attention and go to extremes to fit in — Courtney, for example. Honestly, all those people are doing is robbing themselves of a good time. They should figure out what they enjoy and believe in and do that instead of trying to please everyone else. Trust me, I know from experience. Everyone is different; that's what makes society function. Don't you think God planned it that way for a reason?"

Julianna raised her eyebrows while eyeing Jon skeptically. "I don't know. I don't really believe God planned anything."

Jon laughed. "Oh, okay, so life is just a coincidence?"

"An unfortunate one," Julianna stated and looked down at her feet.

Jon shook his head. "That's a horrible thing to say."

"Oh, so what are you religious or something?" Julianna rebuked. "You don't really strike me as the type."

"I have faith if that's what you mean. Although believing in God is common sense," Jon replied matter-of-factly.

"What do you mean?"

"Well, for one, why am I inside my body and why are you inside yours? Obviously, we have souls," Jon stated matter-of-factly.

"I guess," Julianna said, as if she had never considered the possibility.

"It says in the Bible that God created us from dirt — and yes, I've read the Bible. Scientists recently discovered that the exact elements that make up the human body are the same elements found in common dirt. Now science is trying to take credit for discovering something that was written thousands of years ago. It just shows you how much can be learned from studying God's word."

"I'm sure that would fix my problems," Julianna remarked sarcastically.

"Do you know what I think? You're an emotional mess, and you care way too much about what other people think," Jon stated flatly. "You're wasting your life caring about things that don't even matter."

"They matter to me," Julianna replied.

"Look, girl. If you want to feel better, you need to stop running away from your problems. You're like a dark rain cloud. If you can figure out what you believe in, you'll find the security you're looking for."

"Oh, I'm sure that will help."

"At this point, you've got nothing to lose," Jon said matter-of-factly.

<u>Courtney Angeletti—Saturday</u>
I harshly dismissed Julianna from my life, and I failed to be honest with myself. I lied repeatedly, trying to convince myself that she had changed and that was why we'd grown apart. It worked for a while. I mean I actually forgot she existed—something I am not proud of. But when I found her this morning in the emotional state she was in, I found out more about myself than I ever imagined possible:

1) I am no greater than anyone I have compared myself to.

2) What I have thought has made me only shallow and more insecure than the people I have shunned and ridiculed.

3) I have lost sight of everything important.

I grew up inside a bubble; I had the friends I grew up with, my last name that earned me respect, and the gift of charisma. I never had to put in effort to attain any of those things. Suddenly, I was at MLH where there were new faces, new cliques, and new standards. Subconsciously that did a number on my self-esteem. When I saw how close Alyssa and Cathy were with a lot of the freshmen guys, I felt threatened—just like when I saw how pretty Lisa is. My desire to remain at the top of the social ladder turned me into a superficial person. I'm sure everyone could see that—thank God, I now can.

Jon—the boy I told off for being honest with his feelings—spent the night outside of Chris's house, comforting a girl who meant nothing to him. That should have been me out there, comforting the girl who had been my best friend for a decade.

Instead, I had pushed her down to where she was and left her there to rot. And why? Because I felt the need to be accepted by the popular crowd—a crowd made up of people dying to push each other down so they could be on top. When I thought I belonged on their level, I was more than right. I was there already.

⁂

<u>Julianna Camen—Saturday</u>

When Courtney came running out of Chris's house this morning, Chris, Bryan, Marielle, Chantal, and Chris's cousin followed her. I didn't even look up at any of them. I just kept my eyes glued on Jon. When Courtney threw her arms around me, apologizing for causing me pain, I held my gaze on Jon. I can't believe I spent the night on the street,

143

crying my eyes out in his arms. He must think that I have serious problems! I, on the other hand, think Jon's the sweetest kid I've ever met. Despite how many friends he has, I think I've seen a side of him the others haven't. He was understanding and patient with me. He gave me the support I needed to be honest with my feelings. Jon Anderson made me happy. I'm trying to decide if I should let him know that. But I do know one thing: I'm through with running. I've received something greater than attention. My eyes have been opened to something I had never considered—my life may have a purpose.

<u>Jon Anderson—Saturday</u>

I never fell asleep last night. Instead, I found something inside myself. What I found was the faith I had begun to question still existed.

Chantal and I met at church, we hung out at church, and we centered our relationship on our Christian values. I can't complain—our relationship was amazing. To this day I am shocked she broke up with me, but at the same time I can understand where she was coming from. I started doing things I had always been against. My friends started partying, and I felt the need to keep up with them. I didn't want to lose my friends! The more I partied, the more I lost sight of what was important to me. Then, I eventually lost Chantal. Sadly, I haven't been to church since. So, I ask myself, where has my new life gotten me?

My friends—you know, the ones I sacrificed my morals to keep—I don't even like them anymore. I was bored out of my mind at Jason's party last night. Anyone with eyes or ears could tell you I was incredibly annoyed. I've done my share of partying, but it's just not for me. Not the way they party. Nothing positive comes from it. It's so frustrating to see people I care about giving into peer pressure right in front of me. Last night, I completely snapped. I couldn't take it anymore! I can't live that life any longer, not after comparing it to how great my life once was. That was why I had to give Julianna tough love. She probably wouldn't believe me if I told her I had felt the same way as her two years ago. That was the epiphany I had when I was talking to her last night. It wasn't worth it! None of it was. I never should have sacrificed my own beliefs to fit in. Staying up all night with Julianna was the most unselfish thing I have done in a long time. Funny though, I think I got more than I gave in return.

CHAPTER 23

On Monday morning, Cathy entered the freshman locker hall with Alyssa and locked her eyes on Courtney. "Oh, look. It's the girl who changes boyfriends every week," she said sarcastically and smirked at Alyssa.

Alyssa glanced at Courtney in a disgusted manner.

"Just ignore them, Court," Jon stated loudly as he stood between Courtney and Julianna.

"Alyssa, do you have a problem with me?" Courtney asked, raising her eyebrows in disbelief. "That would be odd, seeing that I was the only one who stood up for you at Jay's."

Alyssa shot her eyes from Jon to Courtney, clearly bothered that Courtney was standing beside him. "I don't know what you're talking about," she replied. "My memory of Friday night is a little blurry."

"Oh, really? Well, that's fine. I guess," Courtney said and walked away.

"Just like that?" Alyssa called down the corridor.

Courtney paused for a second and then continued walking. *Yup. Just like that.*

<u>Marielle Kayne—Monday Night</u>
Finally, things have returned to normal between Court, Julie, and me. Chantal fits in well with us, and her boyfriend Andy seems really nice. Over one weekend, I gained an entire group of friends. I think I'm going to like high school!

"I thought I might find you here," Jon sang, greeting Julianna at his locker on Tuesday morning.

Julianna smiled. "Well, I figured if I stood here long enough, you or Court would show up."

"Well, whose locker are you waiting at? Courtney's or mine?" Jon questioned her as he turned his combination lock.

"Yours," Julianna replied with a twinkle in her blue eyes.

"That's what I like to hear," Jon said with a laugh. "So, what's up?"

"Marielle, Chris, Chantal, and Andy are double dating for the dance next Friday. Courtney and Bryan want us to go with them. I guess they figured we're going together or something. I don't know what made them think that."

147

"Me," Jon admitted and turned to face Julianna. "I told them yesterday that I want to ask you, and Courtney suggested that we all go together. They must have thought I already asked you."

Julianna looked stunned. "You really want to take me to the dance?"

Jon nodded. "As long as you make a habit of hanging out with me more often."

Julianna blushed deeply. "I can do that," she replied.

Chris Dunkin

So, it was an eventful first week of school. I can't honestly guess many of the events will mean anything to me five years from now, but I know the friendships will. If you had asked me a year ago, I probably wouldn't have been able to confidently say that.

It was nice to see Jon's sights on a nice girl like Julianna. Actually, it was nice to see Julianna bring out the caring side of Jon. I hadn't seen that since he and Chantal dated. Then again, Chantal has always had a way of bringing out the best in everyone.

I saw Chantal when I went to church that first time with Courtney. She was there with her parents, her little sister, and Andy. She was shocked to see me! I told her briefly about what happened between Courtney and me during our breakup. She smiled and said God had answered her prayers. I found out that she had been praying since seventh grade for God to find a way to reach me. I knew someone must have been praying for me, and I love Chantal for being that person. I think her prayers got me to Courtney,

Courtney got me to church, and church got me to God.

It was there at the altar, at the end of service on that first Sunday, that I got the strength I needed to straighten out my life. The ironic thing is that I didn't pray for strength specifically—I repented. I put my faith in Christ. It's an experience that words cannot describe, but it is amazing. I think we are all born dead in spirit and can only come alive through making a connection with God. Accepting Jesus Christ as my Savior is the one thing I know I will remember about my first week of high school for the remaining years of my life.

After that Sunday, my desires began to change. I didn't even have to ask God to take them out of my heart. He just did it on His own. That was five months ago. I've been sober ever since.

More Books by Stacy A. Padula

Gripped Part 1: The Truth We Never Told

In high school, Taylor Dunkin broke more records than any other athlete to step foot in Montgomery, Massachusetts. As a sophomore in college, he was ranked by ESPN as one of the NFL's top 100 prospects. However, his aspirations came to a jarring halt when a season-ending injury sent him spiraling into a dark world of pain, depression, and addiction.

One year later, Taylor is a person of interest in a highly confidential investigation headed by the Boston Police Department. He has entangled himself in a crime ring notorious for pushing drugs on local college campuses. Montgomery's hometown hero has fallen hard, and he's taking a lot of people down with him.

Luke Davids has become the middleman between Taylor and teens in Montgomery who want to buy drugs. Freshmen Cathy Kagelli, Chris Dunkin, and Jason Davids are just a few of the students at Montgomery Lake High who have fallen victim to the benzos and opiates supplied by Taylor and Luke.

When Taylor's youngest brother Marc discovers that Taylor is behind the copious amount of pills circulating around his high school, he sets off to not only reverse the damage Taylor has caused, but also save his lifelong role model from becoming a casualty of America's deadly opioid epidemic.

Gripped Part 2: Blindsided

Fourteen-year-old Chris Dunkin is known for being the life of the party and everyone's favorite friend. Despite his amicable nature, he carries around deep-seated pain from his childhood that he frequently numbs with alcohol and drugs.

After hosting a party, Chris awakes with a strange vibe running through his body and no recollection of the previous night. When he learns the horrifying truth of what his night entailed, the trajectory of his life is changed forever.

Gripped Part 3: The Fallout

After a near-death experience, Chris Dunkin begins surrounding himself with positive influences and putting his efforts towards living a clean lifestyle. However, the night before school starts, his best friend Jason convinces him to host a party that shows Chris more about himself than he actually wants to know.

Eighteen-year-old Marc Dunkin has received word from a detective that his oldest brother Taylor is a person of interest in a highly confidential case headed by the Boston Police Department. They know Taylor's clean; they know he wants out of the game; and they want to help make that happen. However, their "help" will come at a cost—one that may put Taylor and his entire family in grave danger.

Twenty-three-year-old Taylor Dunkin is trying to get his life back in order after an opiate addiction wreaked havoc on his once promising athletic future. Getting clean was a difficult feat, but breaking free from the Bilotti crime ring will present an even greater challenge.

Gripped Part 4: Smoke & Mirrors

After spending her first month of high school grounded, Cathy Kagelli is finally allowed to socialize and uncover what her boyfriend, Jason Davids, has been up to without her. When Cathy realizes Jason has been experimenting with a variety of drugs, she devises a plan to save him from himself... but she just may lose herself in the process.

Meanwhile Taylor Dunkin finds himself playing a game with even higher stakes because his life, his reputation, and the safety of everyone he loves are all on the line. Taylor's two younger brothers, Jordan and Marc, have been at odds for years, but they are brought together to decipher the mysterious clues Taylor is leaving regarding his whereabouts. As secrets are revealed, the Dunkin boys' relationships will be changed forever. In Taylor's weakest moment, he made a deal with the devil, and now there is a reckoning. But who will pay the price?

Gripped Part 5: Taylor's Story

Taylor Dunkin is missing.

The last message Jordan Dunkin receives from Taylor leads him to Taylor's abandoned Jeep. Each of Taylor's family members holds a piece of the puzzle, and as the Dunkins begin putting the details together, they are awakened to the possibility they may never see Taylor again.

No one can find Missy Kent.

Missy's boyfriend Luke Davids last saw her dancing with their friends at a nightclub, but she hasn't responded to anyone's texts or calls for hours.

Everything is connected.

Taylor and Missy's friends are dangerously close to learning the truth, but their ignorance might be the only thing keeping them safe. Every clue is leading them closer to peril.

The fifth book in the Gripped series moves through details at a thrilling pace. Secrets are revealed and lives are at stake. Taylor, Missy, their friends, and their families must figure out who they can trust before it's too late.

Montgomery Lake High #2: When Darkness Tries to Hide

Students at Montgomery Lake High believe the ominous clouds and impending storm will only bring a temporary interruption to their regularly scheduled lives. However, when the tempest grows worse and a classmate's life hangs in the balance, students must pull together to support each other and seek help for their friend. As the lines between cliques dissolve, dark secrets are revealed and hearts are transformed.

Montgomery Lake High #3: The Aftermath

At age fifteen, Jason Davids appears to have it all: high grades, popular friends, a beautiful girlfriend, and nearly any worldly thing that promises enjoyment at his disposal. Despite this, there is a persistent emptiness inside his heart. After failing to fill the void with achievements, relationships, and illicit substances, Jason finds himself intrigued by Jessie: a rather quiet girl, who is the daughter of a local pastor. How is it possible that she stands for everything his lifestyle opposes yet possesses the one thing he has been searching for all along?

Montgomery Lake High #4: The Battle for Innocence

Jon Anderson and Chantal Kagelli are trying to live moral lives, but temptations are plaguing them in and out of school. Will they continue to be lights in their best friends' lives or will they get pulled into the darkness?

Montgomery Lake High #5: The Forces Within

After being trapped inside his own body, unable to communicate with anyone but his own thoughts, Andy Rosetti finally wakes up from the coma that controlled his life for one month. But upon awakening, Andy finds himself and his friends in an unfamiliar setting: a mansion riddled with secret passages and supernatural forces. As his friends fall prey to the entities surrounding them, Andy must figure out if the darkness lies within the mansion's walls or within the people surrounding him.

About the Author

Stacy Padula grew up in Pembroke, Massachusetts. She is the founder of Briley & Baxter Publications, the founder of South Shore College Consulting & Tutoring, a co-founder of BLE Pictures, and the author of thirteen books. She began writing her first book series, *Montgomery Lake High*, when she was a teenager because she saw a need for realistic Y.A. books that address topics such as substance abuse and bullying. Between 2010-2014 all five *Montgomery Lake High* books were published. In 2017, she began writing her second series, *Gripped*, which serves as both a prequel and sequel to her first series. *Gripped* parts 1-5 were published between 2019-2021. She is currently writing part 6. In 2019, she also wrote her first screenplay, an adaptation of her novel *The Aftermath*, and worked on writing a pilot for *Gripped*, which caught the attention of Hollywood producers.

In 2020, she began writing a third book series with NBA Coach Brett Gunning. Geared towards children ages three through eight, Stacy and Brett's *On The Right Path* book series has been endorsed by Joel Osteen, Mike D'Antoni, and Kevin McHale as a series that belongs in every school, library, and household. Both Stacy's Gripped series and On the Right Path series are currently being adapted for TV by Emmy award-winning producer Mark Blutman.

Stacy has been featured in Marquis Who's Who in America (2018-Present) for excellence in literature and education, Marquis Who's Who in the World (2018-Present), and Cambridge Who's Who for Young Professionals (2009). In 2018, she was awarded the Albert Nelson Lifetime Achievement Award, and in 2019, the International Association of Top Professionals (IAOTP of New York, NY) chose Stacy as its "Top Educational Consultant of the Year."

In 2020, she was named "Empowered Woman of the Year" by IAOTP and a "Social Impact Hero" by Authority Magazine for her support of animal rescues through her publishing company. She was also chosen to be on the cover of T.I.P. Magazine, an international business publication.

In June of 2021, Stacy was featured on the famous Reuters Building in Times Square as Empowered Woman of the Year. In 2022, she was named "Top Inspirational Author of the Year" and was honored at a gala at the Bellagio in Las Vegas in December. She was also broadcast for her award on the Planet Hollywood Jumbotron overlooking the Las Vegas Strip. Her novel *Gripped Part 5: Taylor's Story* won the Silver Award and *Gripped Part 1: The Truth We Never Told* won the Gold Award for "Best Teen Book" in the 2022 Readers' Choice Awards.

For 2023, Stacy has been named "Top Global Impact Author of the Year" for her literary work on several continents, and she will be honored at a gala at The Plaza in New York City. In addition, she was chosen to be featured in an international publication titled *Top 50 Fearless Leaders*. She also was asked to serve as a judge for the Scholastic Art & Writing Awards, the nation's oldest and most prestigious contest for creative young adults, sponsored by Bloomberg Philanthropies, The New York Times, and Scholastic.

Connect with Us!

Gripped Book Series Instagram @gripped.book.series
Stacy's Instagram @author_stacypadula
Stacy's Twitter @thegrippedbooks
Cathy's Instagram @ckagelli99
Chantal's Instagram @chantal_kagelli
Jason's Instagram @jds_on
Lisa's Instagram @lisa_ankerman99
Chris's Instagram @dunkin_85
Luke's Instagram @lukedavids97
Alyssa's Instagram @alyssa_kelly02
www.stacyapadula.com
www.brileybaxterbooks.com
www.highambition.org

Did You Enjoy MLH #1?

If you loved this book, would you leave a review on Amazon?